Tales of the Quiet Stranger in the Black Hat

Paul John Hausleben

Cover design and cover concept by Paul John Hausleben
All photographs by Paul John Hausleben

Published by God Bless the Keg Publishing
Somewhere, U.S.A.

ISBN: 978-0-990-6979-0-9

This is a work of fiction. Names, characters, businesses, places, events, and incidents are either the product of the author's eccentric, strange and unusual imagination or used in a fictitious manner. Any resemblance to actual persons, living or dead or actual events is purely coincidental, and it was not the intention of the author.

Dedications

For the lost souls of this world, in hopes that a quiet stranger in a black hat appears to help them all along the way

The Cardboard Castle

Eleven Sentences *
(Alternate Ending)

Forever Pensive

The Gypsy

As the Flame Flickers

Dust of the Ages

* Eleven Sentences originally appeared in *The Autumn Collection* by Paul John Hausleben. The selection contained herein, has an alternate ending from the original version.

Contents

Dedication . . . Pg.4

Acknowledgement . . . Pg.7

Preface . . . Pg.9

Prologue . . . Pg.14

The Cardboard Castle . . . Pg.15

Eleven Sentences
(Alternate Ending)

1 - An Old Pub . . . Pg. 33

2 – The Stranger . . . Pg. 48

3 – Five Leaves . . . Pg. 68

4 – A Different Direction . . . Pg. 76

Forever Pensive . . . Pg. 79

The Gypsy . . . Pg. 100

As the Flame Flickers . . . Pg. 124

Dust of the Ages . . . Pg. 147

Epilogue . . . Pg. 167

About the Author . . . Pg. 168

Acknowledgements

Thank you to all the quiet strangers with or without black hats in my own life. Some of them wandered along here and there, and they provided help and inspiration for me to create this character and to make these stories a reality.

"I deal in love, joy, hope, and memories, as well as blowing off the dust of the ages."

Paul John Hausleben
January 2015

Preface from the Author

Many, many years ago, I sat in a classroom staring at an instructor while he reviewed my latest creation that I submitted for a review and his grade. I was a student in a creative writing course for fledgling writers, and this was my first attempt at submitting something other than the usual humorous writings that I typically penned. It was a short story entry, a very short word count requirement, for a mandatory course obligation. Flash fiction, per se.

Not my cup of tea. I am too long-winded.

Observing his face, he clearly was not impressed. After screwing his mouth up like a corkscrew and several other ominous telltale clues of a pending poor review and low grade, he finally spoke up.

"Hausleben, you have some considerable talent, but in reviewing your latest effort here with this dramatic fiction genre, you are not quite yet a tortured soul. To be even a marginal writer of emotion and drama, you have to be a tortured soul. You should consider becoming an alcoholic, or have some gorgeous woman you are infatuated with, destroy your heart and soul by dumping you and running a ramshackle over you. You still harbor too much happiness, too much of that dry sense of humor, which you inherited from your English heritage. You look at life as though it will always turn out right. Life never really does turn out right. All of us old curmudgeons can testify to that fact. The pretty woman never picks guys like you, and when on rare occasions they do, in the end, they ultimately always dump you. Until you feel that pain and emotion, then you need to stick to the humorous genre. Until, you know, until . . . you feel the true pain of life. This story sucks, but you do have a gift for creating a magical setting and wonderful characters, and since I laughed once, even though I was not supposed to, I am going to give you a ninety-five."

Hmm?

I thought at the time; how I was not quite ready to sacrifice my liver or otherwise, take the instructor's rather dubious advice in order to achieve hints at published glory.

Now, years and years later, I feel as if I have been through life's wringer. Tortured is a bloody strong word to use, but despite the pain, I am still thinking as if I might have a bit of a long way to go.

Sure, as hell, I must be creeping a bit closer though.

I sure have the notches on my ass to prove it.

After volumes of Harry and Paul Adventures, and other assorted poppycock, this book is a bit of a change for me. It is the first book that I have written, in which I would fit solely into the fantasy genre. This book also has a central character, who I truly wish that somehow, actually existed in this tired, old world.

Who knows, perhaps, he really does exist.

I have witnessed many strange things in my life and I suspect that I will continue to do so!

Fantasy is a different genre for me to dabble in and this book contains an unusual main character for me to feature. Readers of my past material might be a bit shocked at the radical change in direction on this go around. However, upon closer examination of the subject material, a sharp-eyed reader will see that this book is actually a roundabout of sorts with a trip back in time to one of my original characters.

A character, in which I created a long time ago, and a character whose existence I based upon an actual gentleman that I met, when I was a very young man. We met, while sitting together at a bar, in a gin joint a long time ago. He was an unusual man, and the two of us shared an unusual conversation over some beers. An impressionable young man with the last name of Hausleben, who was seeking his fame and fortune, took it all in and then combined it to create this fantasy character.

It is funny, in this wild ride we all call life, how certain aspects return to us in some shape or form so many years later.

Not long after completing that enigmatic creative writing class, I wrote the rather bizarre story entitled, *Eleven Sentences.* The story, in the original manuscript, was quite a different story than how the final product turned out when I published it in *The Autumn Collection.* I wrote that story a long time ago, and I utilized the man I had met in the gin joint as the inspiration for the story. I put the original manuscript away and never did a thing with it, until I started writing again in 2010 and the story, in a greatly modified form, made an appearance, some thirty-plus years later in *The Autumn Collection.*

The character caused quite a stir as readers probed and questioned me as to whom or what the quiet stranger in the black hat was.

Supposition abounded! Emails and letters poured into the writing post! Was he a spirit, an angel, a ghost, a superhero? Maybe of all of them combined?

Maybe, perhaps, who knows? Nary, a whisper of a hint from the warped mind of the bizarre creator.

Close friends of mine will testify as to how Paul loves his superhero movies and characters. I must confess to being a bit of a comic book buff. When I was young, much to the chagrin of my mom and dad, I wasted quite a bit of allowance earned, or the few, meager pennies that I saved by delivering newspapers, shining shoes, and doing odd jobs, on baseball, football, hockey trading cards and comic books.

I would eagerly grab a new comic book edition, a pack of trading cards, and drop a few hard-earned coins on the counter of Pete's corner candy store (by the way, it was a front for a well-known bookie joint) on Belmont Avenue in Paterson, New Jersey. I would run home to enjoy the latest adventures of my favorite superheroes and search in earnest for that coveted football card of a certain quarterback for my beloved New York Jets, some flamboyant guy who wore mink coats on the sidelines for the Jets. A guy named Joe.

I would think that based upon that strong fascination of superheroes, sporting heroes and fantasy of which, I still have, the common thought or supposition, would be that the quiet stranger in the black hat is some kind of superhero.

Perhaps.

I think it is best to allow the reader to decide who the quiet stranger in the black hat really is, in his or her own manner and imagination. Yes, indeed, it is best to enjoy his identity in your own way. Perhaps someday, I will share with readers my own vision for whom or what; he actually is, at least in the manner of what or how I created him.

Maybe.

Until then, we can all dream together, and hope and pray that when we are in despair, or life's weight is crushing us and the entire world seems to be a quagmire of desperation and hopelessness, that the quiet stranger in the black hat will come along and help all of us when we need it so much.

I do think in searching my own heart that is the actual reason that I wrote this collection and recreated him. He symbolizes that no matter how dire the situation, there is indeed, always someone who cares or some kind of beacon of hope to offer in all of our own lives. I do feel strongly that somewhere in the vast mysteries of this world, there is a character such as the quiet stranger in the black hat. If the character does not exist in the physical presence, then certainly, he must exist within each of our own hearts.

There just has to be a quiet stranger somewhere.

I hope and pray that if you, dear reader, are suffering with some type of conflict or despair that he would take the time to visit you too.

I enjoyed putting together this fantasy compilation, and it is my hope that you enjoy reading this book, as much as I enjoyed the experience of writing it.

Thank you for reading it.

Paul John Hausleben

January 2015

Prologue

The world we all live in is, in reality, cloaked in the unknown. Our purpose of being here, or in fact, our very existence, is often the greatest question of all.

Why?

The smallest phrase with the largest question, of which humankind has always asked since the beginning of time. Everyone seeks answers, some of us in our own quiet way, some of us in outward and profound methods.

Some of us seek the answers in a church or another type of place of worship. Some of us look to find the answer in science, or in facts, or in books, music, or on top of high mountains, or in schools under the tutelage of wise sages.

Others never seek anything at all; they see the answers in the beauty of a sunset or the face of a loved one. That is proof enough that life is worth living.

Then, there are those human beings, out of the billions of people on this planet, who are exceptional.

They do not ask why we are here, but instead they choose to help those struggling with the profound question of their own existence. These are the people who stand out, either by their actions, or by their exceptional and caring souls, for their undeniable willingness to help others.

Without these exceptional people, this world would be a much more difficult place.

Because of these people, and the mystery of why they share so much of their very souls and give back all of their time to the lost of the world, one has to wonder if without their efforts and love, if humankind would even exist at all.

The Cardboard Castle

The cold grip of winter held the city tightly within its grasp.

Cold, dark, foreboding.

A bitter wind whistled between the buildings and tore through the streets and alleys, freezing everything in its path. The wind spared nothing from the harsh chill. No humans, not any animals, nor any trees or plants, or inanimate things. Nothing.

Relentless, powerful, ominous.

The sunset was not discernible; it seemed as if on this day; it had even forgotten to rise.

The man staggered and stumbled from the curb of the street, back towards the buildings. Slow, painful and wandering steps. Putting one foot in front of the other was now a calculated and difficult task. Neon lights from the storefronts lining the city streets were his beacon; they blinked and flashed, guiding him on his way. He was obviously intoxicated, or in fact, blitzed by an excessive intake of alcohol.

The wind tore at him, and passersby avoided his drunken meanderings, while no one spoke a word to him. He struggled against the bitter wind, tilting at the impact of its fury.

He wore an old overcoat that was unbuttoned and open; the wind forcing its will directly upon his body. His hair blew around upon his head in disarray and with no hat upon his head; the cold worked its way inside his very soul, tearing at an empty mind and numb body.

Mindless numbing of an already numb spirit.

The man barely made his way, his head down, a blank stare straight ahead. Dangling precariously in the grasp of his right hand was his only friend . . . a brown bag filled with a bottle of cheap wine. An old backpack, strapped upon his back, held all of his worldly possessions. All that he owned; he could carry in one backpack.

How the mighty have fallen!

When you are this far down, the only consolation is that you cannot fall any further. The bottom of despair is where it all ends.

While he stumbled along, he viewed his final goal through frozen tears and with watery eyes. Yes, he thought, his home was not far away now. A few more steps, a few more turns, and he will finally be there. Even deep within a drunken haze, his only hope was that a truck or city bus did not backfire, or someone here on the streets shouted aloud or some other loud noise came along.

Oh, how he hated diving for cover. . ..

How he hated when he had to go back there again. Where the bullets fly and the mortars explode. That place in Hell.

He needed his castle, his comfort, his home.

The man made one incorrect turn, and he stumbled and stopped when he realized his error. His watery eyes focused, he stared hard into the pending darkness. With this amount of liquid courage in his bloodstream, forward propulsion of a meaningful manner in the correct direction was the trouble. Stopping, stumbling and starting was easy. The man staggered forward; he looked up, turned right, banged into a wall and fell over.

It was a rough one.

He climbed back up on one knee, when a passerby, a young man dressed in a suit, leaned over, put his hand under his shoulder and tugged at him to assist in bringing him back upright.

"C'mon up now, here you go. Steady now, you pitiful drunken bum. Hang on and stay steady," the young man told him while helping him back to his feet. The man looked at his temporary caretaker and he tried hard to smile.

Smiling was something that did not come easy; never did a smile ever come to his face these days.

Not since that wretched day. He had not smiled since then.

The man held onto the bricks in the wall of the building next to him, looked again at his caretaker and mumbled, "Yes, I am good. Thanks."

"Ya sure?"

The man nodded his head, and the young man in the suit loosened his grip on his arm, nodded and waved while turning to be back on his way. The man looked ahead, realized that his home was now only a few hundred feet away, and he turned up a narrow alleyway between two buildings. He slowly stumbled by trash dumpsters, trash cans, an old car seat, a pile of broken glass. He almost stumbled over the edge of an old mattress dumped here long ago.

Typical urban territorial markings.

Still, the wind worked against him, whipping along the sides of the buildings, spinning in a vortex down the alleyway.

There it was . . . his castle!

Still safely tucked next to a set of stairs, wedged between the dumpster for the Chinese restaurant. His castle actually was a large cardboard refrigerator box, with a wooden pallet and plastic for a roof and an old carpet section for a bed.

He bent over, tore the backpack off his back, and tossed it into his castle. He crawled into his humble abode and collapsed, spilling the sad remains of his only friend all over his overcoat. He worked his body into the dirty and disgusting carpet, in which he called his bed, and his only wish was the rats that he shared it with would leave him alone tonight. He hated when they crawled over his face, when he tried to sleep.

There in the stillness of his castle, the man sighed deeply; he pulled his coat around him and shivered. Keeping warm was always the trouble, but at least down here, tucked in this quiet nook, the wind could not get to him. Tonight, it would not matter; the temperature would dip so low that the wind would not be a factor in his demise. Drifting off to sleep was what he needed most of all, and then he would return to the place. . ..

The place in which sent him into this cardboard haven.

This time, he prayed it would be his last trip there and death would be so peaceful. It will be so nice to freeze to death while still hidden within a drunken stupor.

No more pain, no more anguish. He knew, however, that would require him to make one last journey to that place far away, into a distant land.

His friends long ago, when he first returned from his military duty and journey, would often ask him, "When did you leave Vietnam?"

His answer to them was always the same, "Never left. I return there every, single night."

His eyes closed and sleep quickly came over the man.

Surely, in the frigid temperatures of the rapidly approaching winter night, freezing to death was now a distinct possibility and he would only have to visit Vietnam one last time.

"Bordon! Over here! Over here, Bordon! I am hit!" Private First-Class Robinson cried out.

Specialist Fourth Class Laurence Bordon kept his head down low as the bullets and mayhem whistled over his head. He could hear his best friend, Private First-Class Carl

Robinson, crying out for help and he knew that he was only a few feet away. If only he could climb out of this trench and reach him. He had to save him!

Specialist Fourth Class, Laurence Bordon, twenty-two years old, from the Bunker Hill section of Paterson, New Jersey, B Company, 2nd battalion, 27th INF, 25th Infantry Division, of the United States Army Reserve, leaned back into the side of the foxhole. He adjusted the pot on his head and jammed his jungle boots into the dirt on the other side of the hole. Explosions were all around them, bullets whistling in all directions, rockets in the air, lights and fire all around, all of it blinding him as it was flashing in his eyes.

His chest heaved in anguish, his body trembled, and blood poured from a head wound.

Hell was all around him.

If only he could put his head up for a second, grab The Pig, and stick it over the side and fire. He tugged at the M-60. Timing was going to be the key factor here; he still could hear the cries for help, and it tore at his very soul.

He screamed aloud, "Damn! Shit, man! I gotta save, Carl. How in the hell did I ever end up here? Deep breath Bordon, deep breath, ya are a Paterson, New Jersey street kid, ya been in worse spots. Let's go get 'em!"

Specialist Fourth Class Bordon pulled the M-60 up, and in one gallant effort of superhuman strength and courage, he set it on the edge of the foxhole, while simultaneously squeezing the trigger. His only fear now was that the humidity of this godforsaken place would cause The Pig to malfunction.

Specialist Fourth Class Bordon was a very strong man, built as if he was a solid rock and he was going to need all of that power, and perhaps, a touch of the hand of God too.

He had linked two-hundred rounds to this baby and fire he did. He fired as if he was a wild man, and when the enemy, due to his efforts, stalled in their advance, he jumped out of the hole and pulled at the M-60 to place it in front of him. He screamed at the top of his lungs and while running as fast as he could; he continued to fire, while never stopping his screaming!

He mowed the enemy down as if they were bowling pins; he fired blindly and wildly, until all he remembered was a flash of light, a concussion of noise, which blew his eardrums out and he found himself five feet in the air, spinning around and around, toppling over himself in the air. Still, somehow, he held onto his weapon and remarkably; he fired until he landed and hit the ground with a thud.

He thought that he was dead.

'It was so peaceful,' he thought, 'What had he been afraid of? Death was so easy.'

He woke up in a hospital bed and he stared around the room.

A pretty nurse was standing at the foot of his bed. She smiled at him and said, "Welcome back, soldier. You are my hero and a lot of other people's hero too."

A purple heart was pinned to his pillow and when he finally recovered, they pinned The Silver Star Medal on his chest.

The documentation for the medal explained that, "The President of the United States of America, authorized by Act of Congress 09 July 1918, (amended by an act of 25 July 1963) takes pride in presenting the awarding of The Silver Star Medal to Specialist Fourth Class, Laurence Bordon. In an unwavering moment of extreme gallantry, on 24 July 1968, despite severe wounds of his own, Specialist Fourth Class, Laurence Bordon, B Company, 2nd battalion, 27th INF, 25th Infantry Division, of the United States Army Reserve, single-handedly repelled an enemy ambush, which was overwhelming a battalion of United States forces in Tay Ninh Province, the Republic of South Vietnam. His brave actions neutralized twenty-two enemies of the United States of America and saved the lives of twelve of his fellow soldiers in arms. His country awards him, for his gallantry in combat against enemies of the United States of America, The Silver Star Medal."

Many of his comrades thought it should have been The Medal of Honor or at least, The Cross. Poor guys from Paterson, New Jersey fighting in the most unpopular of wars, well, they do not receive those medals.

The hero eventually went home, with his medals, with his memories and with the ghosts that haunted him every day and every night. Sweat-filled nightmares of cries for help, explosions in his ears, bullets and rockets, flying all around him, then that feeling of spinning in the air and that peaceful feeling of death.

Home, to a marriage that fell apart, home to quivering in dark closets and corners in dingy apartments, trembling in fear when a loud noise occurred outside his window upon the city streets, home to no jobs, people who spit on him, cursed at him and called him a "Baby killer." The veterans from the big wars returned as heroes. The veterans from Vietnam returned to ridicule, despair and a nation of citizens who turned their backs to them.

Home, where the bottle became his best friend. Where his family abandoned him and where rehabilitation failed and his friends forgot.

In addition, his country forgot too.

The very country in which pinned the medals upon his chest and sent him home now abandoned him at the time when he needed help the most.

He started a long, downward spiral, which seems as if it will culminate in a frozen body on this cold, winter night in this sad cardboard box.

Just another statistic in an unforgiving city.

On the other hand, was he?

Five city blocks away from the cardboard castle of Laurence Bordon, out upon that same city street, in which

Laurence had previously made his way, a very different man strode along the city streets.

He walked quickly, his long, lean frame covering the ground in wide strides. The bitter wind blew hard against this man, too, as it did so many others on this harsh and brutal winter day, which was now rapidly turning into an unforgiving nighttime. There was a difference though, because to this man the brutal wind had no ill effect. As cold and as bitter as the wind was and no matter how hard it blew, the man was impervious to the bitterness.

He was dressed all in black, with sharply creased black trousers, and a black shirt, and all he wore as extra protection against the cold was a black leather vest. A vest that despite the brutally cold weather and wind, he left unbuttoned except for the last button before his waist. On his head was a black hat with a wide brim, which he pulled down close to his ears, but you could still make out some of his facial features.

On his feet were black, sharp-tipped boots, with metal clips on the edges that made a distinct clicking noise as he walked along the cold sidewalk. A neatly trimmed, black beard framed his handsome face and his facial features were striking, with a trimmed moustache that neatly lined his mouth.

He walked with an air of confidence as he strode along. Everyone who noticed him could tell that this was a gentleman that was used to traveling around, and you could easily see that he was comfortable in many different surroundings. A busy city sidewalk meant nothing to him while he easily navigated the wind and dodged between the rushes of humanity.

He had dark, black, piercing eyes that focused straight ahead and his eyes did not move or even glance at the many pedestrians who stared at him. His face was void of expression; he had no emotions, and an aura of an ominous presence surrounded him.

It seemed as if he had a mission, in which nothing could derail.

Even in this terrible weather, where all people had on their minds was seeking an escape from the cold to find warmth, this man caused people to stop and stare at him while he briskly walked along. Women passing by him stole glances at his handsome face. They whispered, "Hello" and they smiled, only to receive no response back from the man. Both men and women stole more than just a glancing stare. One could not help but to be surprised at how all that he was wearing to combat the cold was a hat and a vest on such an awful winter day.

He did not stop; he did not speak; he did not move his eyes, nor did he acknowledge anyone or anything.

He was the quiet stranger in the black hat.

The quiet stranger simply walked briskly along, until he reached that same dark, dismal alley where a man, or perhaps, a better description would be that it was an alley where you could find a hero sleeping inside of a cardboard box.

The quiet stranger stopped at the opening to the alley. He looked around, up and down the alley, and back out to the city street, and after seemingly confirming his final destination, he moved quickly and made his way down the long alley, until finally stopping next to the "doorway" of the cardboard box.

He bent over, knelt down, and peered inside the box to find the half-frozen hero shivering in his drunken stupor while lying on top of the carpet.

The quiet stranger in the black hat reached for the empty bottle of wine and moved it aside. He then reached for the hero and started to shake him violently.

Deep inside of a haze and stupor, the hero left behind Tay Ninh Province within the Republic of South Vietnam.

The hero opened his eyes.

He tried hard to focus, and to see whom or what was

causing him to awaken and avoid such a peaceful and quiet death. A death he dreamed about for so long. A death which would finally end all of his madness.

The hero stared directly into the dark, black, piercing eyes of the quiet stranger in the black hat. Eyes, which penetrated a mind full of alcohol-induced haze and even in a stupor, the hero felt his spine rippling. He never looked into eyes such as these before, not these kinds of eyes. They were dark, quiet, and ominous.

At first, he thought he *was* dead, and this man was some type of angel, or a guardian of Heaven, or even Hell.

In the cold darkness, the hero studied his handsome face; he again looked at his eyes. He looked at his black hat, the vest, the immaculate clothes and his highly polished boots.

I must be dreaming, the hero thought.

The quiet stranger continued to shake at him and tug to arouse the hero, but the hero resisted.

"Leave me alone. Let me die in peace here if I am not dead already! If you are talking to me, speak up, I don't hear so well. Those damn rockets blew my eardrums out in Vietnam."

Resistance was futile.

The quiet stranger in the black hat, in a powerful display of strength, pulled the hero out of the box in one strong lurch and stood him upon his feet.

The hero could not fight back, he was powerless to the quiet stranger's strength, and the hero was a large man himself!

The power of this quiet man took the hero by surprise, and he stood there shaking and stumbling, trying hard to adjust to now being upright.

As he stood there, wavering and wobbling in the freezing cold, the hero said, "Please, take whatever it is that you want. I have nothing to give, please leave me alone. I want to die tonight in this cardboard box."

The quiet stranger, who had yet to utter a single word, placed his powerful hands on the shoulders of the hero to steady him, and he held him upright.

He looked deeply into the hero's eyes and said in a low, powerful voice, "Heroes do not die in cardboard boxes. Come with me."

"Why should I? Please, tell me, why?"

The quiet stranger in the black hat bent down. He reached into the box and pulled the backpack out of the confines of the hero's cardboard castle.

He stood back up, slung the backpack over his shoulder, and then reached into a pocket on the front of his vest. Without saying a single word, the quiet stranger pulled a number of photographs from his vest pocket and he handed them to the hero. The hero received them gently, yet precariously. He was not exactly sure what this stack of photographs had to do with him or what they meant. He looked at the photos in his hand and then back to the face of the quiet stranger, who nodded as if to indicate that the hero should begin to look at the photographs.

The hero steadied himself, pulled the wrap of his overcoat around him, and still he shivered in the cold. There in the darkness, he focused his beleaguered and shipwrecked eyes upon the photographs and viewed them one by one.

There were pictures of smiling women holding hands with handsome, smiling young men. There were wedding pictures of brides and grooms, all people who the hero did not recognize. There were pictures of babies and families posing together while they all were smiling widely in front of glowing Christmas trees. Pictures of children blowing out candles on birthday cakes while families clapped happily in the background. There were photos of young children laughing, riding bicycles, playing baseball, children running and playing with dogs, while chasing each other around in backyards. Pictures of proud mothers and fathers holding newborn infants and perhaps, the most touching photo of all, was one picture of a smiling young man graduating college while holding up a sign that read, "Now onward and upward to medical school!"

The hero did not understand, nor did he know what all of this was for, or who all of these people were in this collection of printed memories.

The hero shook his head back and forth as if to indicate how confused he was, and he handed the photographs back for the quiet stranger in the black hat to take in his hand while saying, "Nice, but it does not mean anything to me. I do not know any of those people. They are all strangers to me! Just as you are! Who are these people? Who in the hell are you? Exactly who do you think you are by coming here and giving me these photos?"

The quiet stranger waved his hand in the air to indicate that he would not take the photographs back; he pointed his finger towards the hero to indicate that he should retain them. The hero was not going to argue with this silent and ominous stranger. Therefore, he tucked them down inside one of the pockets of his tattered overcoat.

When the stranger saw that the hero had followed his gestures, the quiet stranger in the black hat finally spoke, "Those are the wives, girlfriends, children, families, relatives, grandchildren, and memories, of the men whose lives you saved on the twenty-fourth of July in nineteen sixty-eight in Tay Ninh Province, within the Republic of South Vietnam. Without your heroism, none of those photographs would exist. Some of those people would not even have been born, those pictures could not exist, the dreams, enjoyment and memories never recorded. All that joy, all of that happiness, all of those lives—vanquished."

The hero was stunned, and even in his drunken and nearly frozen state, he could fathom the profound impact of what the quiet stranger had just told him.

The profound thoughts staggered him, both physically

and emotionally.

The hero could no longer stand up. His legs gave out from under his body and before he could fully collapse, the quiet stranger captured him in his arms and held him safely.

The quiet stranger in the black hat carried the hero down the alley, down to the city sidewalk and he stood on the curb, holding the hero in his powerful arms, while watching the traffic zip by them.

Among stares of horror from nearby pedestrians, the quiet stranger continued to hold the hero up and when he spotted a city police car rolling down the street, the quiet stranger stepped out into the road to flag the police car down. The police car screeched to a halt, and one of the policemen jumped out to assist the quiet stranger. While rushing over to assist him, the policeman looked the quiet stranger up and down, aghast at the stranger's meager attire on this bitterly cold day.

"Geez . . . pal, where did you find this guy? You know, ya need to be wearing more than just a vest and that hat out here tonight. You are gonna freeze to death too. We will call an ambulance," the policeman said, as his partner jumped out of the driver's side to render assistance.

The quiet stranger looked at the policeman and said, "No, please, take him to the nearest hospital as quickly as you can. He requires immediate medical assistance."

The policeman shook his head and said, "Nah, man, we have to call an ambulance. Why should we?"

The policeman stopped in mid-speech. The piercing eyes of the quiet stranger in the black hat forced him to stop. He dared not say anything else as he met the gaze of the stranger and the policeman studied his face for a few seconds. The stranger's face was void of expression; he had no emotions, and an aura of an ominous presence surrounded him.

Ominous, but commanding.

The policeman was not going to argue with the quiet stranger anymore and the policeman and his partner, first watched in bewilderment, and then they assisted, while the quiet stranger opened the rear door of the patrol car and gently placed the hero in the back seat. No one said a word as the quiet stranger reached inside of the backpack and he pulled out an envelope and some military medals.

He handed them to the policeman, along with the backpack and a large stack of money that he pulled out of his vest, and said, "Why? Because, heroes do not die in cardboard boxes. That is why. Take him to the nearest hospital now. This cash will pay for his medical care and sustain him for a period of time. I strongly suggest the hospital right around the corner from here."

Dr. Carl Robinson Junior was on duty in the hospital emergency room, working the late shift once again.

He asked the emergency room nurse, "So, who or what is up next? Geez, this has been a long shift! Outside tonight, you know, wow, it is so cold and gloomy out there. I think people's spirits are down! Hopefully, the cold keeps people off the streets and the gun battles and knife fights will not occur with the usual frequency this evening!"

The nurse nodded her head in agreement while she handed him a chart on a clipboard. Dr. Robinson Junior rather mindlessly glanced at it.

"Oh geez, more homeless drunks. Drunks who are half-frozen, half-dead, and who cannot pay their bills! What is wrong with this one? How are his vitals?"

The nurse looked up and said, "He is stable now. He was close to hypothermia, but he is warm now. He is still a bit intoxicated and not in good shape, but much better than he was when he first came in, that is for sure. He was half-frozen, but he should make it now. This case is a bit unusual. Not our usual, homeless drunk from the streets. Two policemen brought him in. They said that some stranger . . . a Good Samaritan of sorts found him on the street and saved his life."

"Oh yeah? Okay, well, this is interesting."

"He can pay the bill, too. The policeman said the stranger gave them a wad of cash to pay this bill with, and then some. His coat pockets had all kinds of family photographs stuffed in them. They also brought in a number of military medals, and the two policemen insisted on pinning them to the homeless man's pillow. Weird. Faded photographs, spent memories, cash and military medals, all inside a dirty backpack. His clothes on his back—that is all this guy has left in life. Sad, how far some folks fall."

Doctor Robinson Junior looked at the nurse somewhat puzzled and he said, "Let's take a look. A military man, huh? I wonder why they did not bring him to the Veterans Hospital. It is not too far from here."

The nurse followed Dr. Robinson Junior over to the hero's bedside and he stared at the hero in the bed, who was now sound asleep.

"Doctor, they also gave me this paper. They said the stranger who saved him gave it to them, along with the medals, cash, and that backpack. It is interesting. You should read it. It is about how he won those medals. The policemen also told me not to let this man die because heroes do not die in cardboard boxes."

Doctor Robinson Junior took the tattered paper, gently unfolded it, smiled, and began to read it aloud.

The documentation for the medal explained that, "The President of the United States of America, authorized by Act of Congress 09 July 1918, (amended by an act of 25 July 1963) takes pride in presenting the awarding of The Silver Star Medal to Specialist Fourth Class, Laurence Bordon. In an unwavering moment of extreme gallantry, on 24 July 1968, despite severe wounds of his own, Specialist Fourth Class, Laurence Bordon, B Company, 2nd battalion, 27th INF, 25th Infantry Division, of the United States Army

Reserve, single handedly repelled an enemy ambush, which was overwhelming a battalion of United States forces in Tay Ninh Province, the Republic of South Vietnam. His brave actions neutralized twenty-two enemies of the United States of America and saved the lives of twelve of his fellow soldiers in arms. His country awards him, for his gallantry in combat against enemies of the United States of America, The Silver Star Medal."

When he finished reading, Doctor Carl Robinson Junior dropped the paper in shock. He grabbed a hold of the nurse's arm and steadied himself while he whispered as if he was in shock, "Oh, dear Lord in Heaven!"

"Doctor, doctor, doctor! Are you okay? Doctor Robinson, what is wrong?"

One year or so later, Mr. Laurence Bordon walked out the front door of the Veterans Hospital to catch the city bus to arrive home. He was leaving his job at the hospital where he now worked rehabilitating and counseling homeless veterans, assisting veterans addicted to alcohol or narcotics and veterans who were suffering from combat-related, Post Traumatic Stress Disorder. He was indeed well suited for the position. While he waited for the bus, he suddenly had a strong urge to walk a few blocks over and check out a place, which he had not been courageous enough to visit in over a year.

He looked at his watch and whispered, "I have time. She will understand if I am a little late for dinner." He walked pensively, deep thoughts and pain leaving his body, and soon enough, he stood at the foot of that dark and dreary alley.

The former location of the box.

The cardboard castle.

He stood there for a long time, some tears running down his cheeks, when he suddenly felt a gentle tap on his shoulder. He turned around to stare once again into the eyes of the quiet stranger in the black hat. Laurence was, for some reason, not at all surprised that the stranger would have arrived here to meet him today. The quiet stranger locked his deep, piercing eyes upon Laurence and he smiled. Laurence smiled back. These days, he could rather easily smile again.

"I imagine you will not tell me exactly who you are, and I would think it is best that way—to leave it to my own supposition. My guardian angel, my kindred spirit, or a messenger from Heaven. Who the hell knows? You might even be a manifestation or a projection of my own consciousness! You just had the courage that I did not have, and you cared enough, to make me face what I was too afraid to confront. I dunno, maybe you are someone I contracted with, to share my soul and spirit with. Whatever it is, I have to say that it all works for me. I do need to thank you, for restoring my soul and saving my life."

The quiet stranger said not a word, but he nodded his head and remained smiling.

"Thank you, stranger. I owe you a great debt. I guess your mission is to save old soldiers from their own demons."

The quiet stranger in the black hat finally spoke, and he said, "No, you do not owe me anything. The only demons are the ones we invite to enter our hearts. The world owes all heroes such as you are, something wonderful to repay their willingness to sacrifice everything for a cause, a mission, in which they believe is right, just and kind, or to save their fellow man from an early visit to the very gates of Heaven, or in some cases, Hell. I make sure that the world pays part of that debt back and when it does finally come time for heroes to leave this world, I make sure they do so with the dignity and the respect, in which they earned."

When he finished speaking, he smiled once again, tipped his hat, turned, and walked briskly away.

Laurence stood there for a very long time, watching and

listening, until the quiet stranger in the black hat disappeared from his vision, he was lost in a maze of humanity within the city and he could no longer hear the click of the metal tips of his boots on the walkway.

Laurence smiled, and he softly spoke, "Yes, now I too, make sure that heroes do not die in cardboard boxes."

THE END

Eleven Sentences
(Alternate Ending)

1

An Old Pub

I think that at one time or another, in all of our lives, certain unusual situations come along that at first glimpse, you just cannot understand. They seem at first glance to be normal, or a chance coincidence, and then upon further examination or study, we cannot explain them. Occasional instances occur during all of our lives that contain a mystery, an unexplained twist of fate, an encounter with strange or different people, or a bizarre or unexplained turn of events. It is something that I am very sure all of us have experienced, and when you take the time to look back upon it, you have sometimes wondered from where it all came.

I am no exception.

I had just finished an ice hockey game in Concord, New Hampshire. Concord was one of my favorite places on Earth, a clean New England city that most areas of the country would consider a town. I enjoyed it for the people, for the climate, and the general atmosphere. I may have been born and raised in northern New Jersey, but I really enjoyed visiting and playing professional ice hockey in New England quite a bit. While you could never remove my New Jersey accent, my poor grammar, street slang, and other elements of New Jersey from me, I think I was becoming an adopted New Englander.

We had won a hard-fought battle in a late Saturday afternoon hockey game, with a team from New Hampshire. They did not have a good record, but they certainly were no pushovers. They had battled my team; the Albany Flying Dutchman, tooth and nail, and in the end, we pulled out a three to one victory.

I was physically a little worn from the game, some bumps and some bruises, but I was used to that. It was still early in the season, and by the end of the year, I would be a lot more beat up than I was right now. I had escaped this game without any cuts or stitches, which for a hockey goaltender was always a bonus.

The actual source of my pain and trouble was that I just did not emotionally feel very good right now. Playing a hockey game always lifted my spirits up. It let me forget some recent past and dulled the little ache that was inside of me all the time these days. An ache caused by a common issue for young guys such as I was. I was missing a gal . . . not an ordinary gal, but in my heart, she was the only gal.

Yet, there was just something about being an ice hockey goaltender that lifted me up. It was the challenge; it was the exhilaration; it was the thrill of a save, and it was the sweat running off my mask. It made me forget the loneliness and the pain. It made me forget her face, her smile, and her beauty. The trouble was that after the game ended, it all came back.

As I dressed in my civilian clothes after the game and after taking a shower, I replayed the one goal that I had allowed in my mind over and over. Ordinarily, I did not dwell upon goals that I had allowed, but as of late, I had placed some demanding standards upon my performance. The goal that I allowed started out as a hard slap shot from the point through a screen, which an opposition player then tipped about halfway to the goal. I had gotten down low on the ice when I heard the shot take off, and despite the tip, I had tracked it. When the player tipped the puck in front of the net, it changed direction. But I had come out just past the top of the crease to cut down the angle. I had followed the flight of the shot, and watched as the puck hit me just above my right elbow, and glanced off my shoulder pad. The force of the shot caused the puck to flip and flop, and it spun off my body and leaped towards the net. I spun around, because; I knew that the puck was heading for a goal, and despite my last second lunge, it had just enough momentum to trickle across the goal line.

It would have been a spectacular save, but it was a save that I had made a million times before. I swept the puck out of the net in disgust at my performance as my teammates provided encouragement.

"C'mon Paul John Henson, number twenty-seven, for the Albany Flying Dutchman!" I screamed at myself.

As I said, I always shook off goals scored on me rather quickly, but this one, for some unknown reason, really bothered me. I was mad at myself. I had just made a close game closer, and I should have made the save. Then again, you cannot make all the saves all the time.

I had learned that.

It was the first day of November in 1980; All Saint's Day, to us Lutherans, to many others; it was just the day after Halloween. It was also that strange time of year when Thanksgiving and Christmas loomed on the horizon and you have cold nights and warm days. It was as if nature could not decide which way to go.

I had been with the Albany team for about two months or so, and I was doing quite well. Currently, our team was battling for first place with a team from Maine and a Vermont team. I was leading the league in goaltending stats, and my coach, my teammates, and the general manager were all very pleased with my performance. They had paid me a lot of extra dollars to have me sign a contract here, and they had outbid a number of teams for my services. Being very honest, the money was nice, but I had chosen the Albany hockey club for their location as much as any other deciding factor.

I loved upstate New York. I also enjoyed the circuit that

we traveled for games, and the bonus for me was that I could be home in a few hours to visit my family and friends. My family, friends, and my best buddy in the entire world, Harry M. Redmond Jr., and his new wife Sky Blu Redmond, were a big part of my life, as was my friend, Ms. Rose Rose. It was always nice, if I had a break in the schedule, and some free time, to leave, check in with them, and hang out in New Jersey for a few days. It was difficult, and very lonely being out on my own, and the strange, sudden breakup of my relationship with my true love, Ms. Binky Hobnobber, had left me in a little bit of a bad way. I was working through it, and hockey was my escape.

The hockey club climbed back in the team bus and we all took a short ride back to the hotel where we were staying. It was a loud and jovial ride back to the hotel, as we all were quite pleased with the hard-fought victory. I could hear the "pop" of cold beer cans being opened on the bus in celebration of the win.

Teammates on a hockey club typically stereotyped the team goaltender, and considered them an eccentric, solitary figure, who generally was a loner. Your teammates expected the goaltender to study shooting angles, geometry, opposition's wrist and slap shots, and other in-depth studies of the intricacies of the game of ice hockey.

I was not that type of goalie. I freewheeled every game.

I enjoyed my teammates, and even though I was new on the Albany Flying Dutchman team this year, I had already made many friends on the hockey club. They joked around with me, teased me about my long-haired, hippie lifestyle, and my very different, hard, northern New Jersey accent.

When we arrived in the hotel lobby, the head coach gave us a short speech on how well we played, cautioned us to stay focused, since it was a long season, and then let us ride for the night.

"Say, Rick, you want to go over with me to that Irish pub we went to last time we were here in Concord?" I asked my best defenseman and buddy on the Flying Dutchman, Rick Tremblay. Rick was a bruiser. He was a tall, strong, lanky defenseman, who was a fearless shot blocker. He had a long reach, and he was one tough guy to beat on the ice. His style of play reminded me very much of my boyhood buddy, Jeff Porter. The three of us, Harry, Jeff, and me, played street hockey together on a dead-end street we named "Geyer Street Gardens" in our hometown a long time ago.

Rick was from Ontario Province in Canada and he was a star on our team. He was also a very funny man, who was a great guy to hang out with and share some good times with. Goaltenders, usually attached to, and were fond of their defensive corps, who played in front of them. Defensemen were your initial protectors on the ice and in a strange way off the ice too. When off the ice and not playing, a goalie would try to keep the defense motivated, and whenever you could, you would hang out with them; buy them some beer, food, and other motivators. It was in your best interest, as they were your guys, much the same as an offensive line protects the quarterback in football.

"Sorry, twenty-seven. I promise that we will go together next time we are in Concord. I am going to eat quickly here in the hotel, and then I have to go up to my room, to have a long, weepy-eyed telephone call with my gal back in Oshawa, because she misses me. I have to make believe that I am very sad and upset too at being away from her for so long. I hope you understand. You know how women are, eh?"

I patted him on the back, smiled, and told him, "I understand, Rick. Hey, whip up a quick set of tears. Maybe think about the pain of blocking that shot in the second period."

"Thanks, Paul. I think that is a good idea!"

I bid him a nice evening and went up to my room to pick up some cash and other items. I was back down to the lobby and out the front door in a flash. The pub was within walking distance of the hotel. Rick and I had stumbled upon it on our first game in Concord earlier in the season. It was just a small, family-owned pub operated by an Irish family. I actually had forgotten the name of the pub and just referred to it as the "Irish pub." However, it did have an actual name. I walked briskly, as I remembered the way to the pub. It was just a few short blocks and some twists and turns from the front door of the hotel in downtown Concord.

There were very few things in life that I enjoyed more than a brisk walk on a cold autumn night in New England. It stirred my soul, lifted my spirits, and made me forget whatever was gnawing at me so deeply these days.

The game that we had just finished playing had been an early game, for some type of giveaway promotion for the New Hampshire team, so it was not very late at night now. I knew that I still had a chance to catch the end of the Boston Bears hockey game on the television at the pub. I grew up a New York Rovers fan, but many rungs up the ladder, the Boston Bears held my contract. I figured I had better start watching the club that within a year or so, I hoped to be a part of, and be the starting goaltender for a long, long time.

It had been a clear day with just a few small puffy clouds, which had engaged in a game of hide and seek with the sun, while the afternoon had whiled away. Now, the clear skies of the day had given way to darkness that seemed, for some reason, to come extra slowly upon Concord today.

The nights in northern New England this time of the year could be very cold, as winter loomed right around the corner, ready to roll in like a freight train with snow, ice, and bitter chills. Before the game had started, I could sense the cold nighttime air creeping in during the day, and now I imagined the locals had agreed with me. They knew this would be one of the coldest nights of the autumn season so far because there was not another person moving around while I walked the streets alone towards the pub.

The wind had now changed around and moved in from the northwest; bringing cold air from high up in the mountains and the Canadian border to sweep around the town. As I walked, I could smell the telltale odor of the smoke of wood fires being set in fireplaces and stoves in the houses that lined the old streets. To me, this was a wonderful smell, which foretold of winter days to come. It filled the nighttime air with puffs of smoke that I could see rising above some housetops.

If Concord had been similar to some of our other recent stops along the hockey circuit, or as it had been in Albany, then a few weeks ago, this city had been ablaze in beautiful, fall foliage colors, framing the landscape in a picture, postcard beauty. What had been a fantastic display of an autumn tapestry of color with the famous New England foliage season, now had given way to bare trees and trunks, with only the stubborn oak trees clinging to dried, brown leaves that shook and rattled a dry cry in the cold night air.

Piles of spent, dried leaves gathered along the street where I was walking. They chased each other into corners and tumbled over one another in an endless game of chase, which would continue on, until the snows of winter appeared to freeze them and stop their journey.

I turned from the main street and walked onto a side street. In front of me was a long row of shops and stores. Most of these were older brick buildings, and I could see that most of them were converted mills and small factories. These types of buildings were distinct leftovers from a bygone era, when manufacturing everything from parts for machines, to gloves, hats, boots, and shoes; drove this area's economy. At one time or another, this area manufactured virtually everything you could ever imagine.

Manufacturing built the local economy and now, the old buildings either housed residential apartments or were vacant.

This part of the city was not unlike my own home city of Paterson, New Jersey. The old mills and abandoned factories reminded me of my old neighborhood in Paterson, which was an old city that had at one time harbored a large silk and weaving manufacturing business. That business was the reason that actually brought my mother's side of the family to this country in search of work from England after the big war.

I walked around the last corner and there was the Irish pub right in front of me. I had to guess the pub to be an older building, built in the nineteen forties or so, when this section of the city had been thriving with workers, from one of the now closed down nearby mills. It was constructed of red clay brick, and it had frosted, glass block windows in the front that were all stained and milky from not being cleaned or maintained in many years.

It had a sad, smutty look to it—almost as though it came from some long lost, departed era. The front door was a heavy, old, oak door, with faded paint and lots of chips and dents from many customers and deliveries which had passed through the doors. The front step up from the sidewalk into the pub was steep and much higher in a dimension than an ordinary step. Carved from a large chunk of New Hampshire granite, it now was a reminder of the era of the building of the pub, when construction standards were not worried about, nor were they of any concern.

In one of the front windows was a sad, blinking, neon sign, which slowly blinked, "OPEN" with the letter "N," barely lit. The sign, imprinted with the pub's name, hung on a rusty steel frame directly over the front door. It was a faded metal sign with remnants of a four-leaf clover logo that I could barely read or make out in the darkness. There was a single light bulb that hung on a black iron gooseneck above the sign, but the dimly lit fixture did not help me to read the sign.

As I walked closer, and stood under the sign, I read the name aloud to myself, so that I could remember it for my next visit, "Murphy's Irish Public House." The sign swung in time to the wind and chirped a squeaky melody to the beat of the wind currents.

Those stubborn leaves continued to follow me right up to the front door of the pub, and they chased me right up and into the front door of the establishment.

I reached the front door, stepped up, and covered the large front granite step with one stride, turned the brass doorknob, and walked into the pub. The pub was crowded, and it was loud from the individual conversations going on at the tables. Local folks filled the tables along with what appeared to be relaxed, regular patrons.

The pub was large and wide open. It had a small music stage for bands on my right side, directly inside the front door. There were not any musicians playing now, but a single stool sat in the center of the music stage, with an acoustic guitar leaning up against it. The bar lined the entire back section of the pub, and ran wall to wall, with a mirror mounted on the back wall and the seating areas in front of it.

The hockey game from Boston was playing on the television mounted above the corner of the bar, and a few fans sat at the bar and in tables around the television, while they stared up at the screen, watching the game intently.

I walked up a long center aisle that ran between rows of tables set on each side of the pub. On the far-left side, as I walked towards the bar, were wooden booths that lined one wall from the bar to the front door of the pub.

Quite a few of the patrons and diners turned around when I walked in and looked my way. Some patrons went back to what they were doing, but a few folks stared at me for a while as I made my way towards the bar. I knew that most of these folks were regular patrons of Murphy's, and I am sure they did not see very many strangers in this small hole in the wall in the corner of the old city. That fact, combined with my long-haired, hippie appearance, my casual attire of a tee shirt with the name of my favorite rock-and-roll band, No Way stamped on it, and my canvas sneakers on my feet, all of which combined to make me a fish out of water.

I did not wear an overcoat, just my vest that I wore on most cold days. I have always disliked heavy overcoats and enjoyed the cold weather. I am sure not many people would have guessed my profession, nor what had brought me to this little city, and I rather enjoyed it that way.

Although I was a social and polite person, I very much enjoyed keeping to myself. I was used to it now.

A few men nodded at me. One chap stared for quite a while, and looked slightly upset at my appearance, which was another common occurrence for me to encounter.

As I approached the bar, there was a table, which had four young ladies seated around it. One of them was a very pretty gal, with long brown hair and a nice smile. She stared at me as I came closer, and she smiled at me. I nodded and smiled back, and she looked a little disappointed when I passed them by, and continued towards the end of the bar, which had a few open stools. I was not getting involved in any female adventures these days.

Not on the road, that was for sure.

I had not dated any women since my girlfriend Binky had decided to end our relationship, and she had taken off for university on the west coast. The opportunity was there, but my motivation was not. I had a next-door neighbor back in Albany, who lived about two or three apartments away from me. She was always circling around and flirting with me. I was polite and friendly to her, but never allowed it to go any farther than sharing a few beers or a cup of coffee on the back porch of our apartment.

I needed to concentrate on my hockey career, and I wanted nothing to do with relationships right now. I also knew in my heart that I was not over Binky. In fact, maybe I never would be.

I sat near the end of the bar, a location close to where it curled around towards the rear-mirrored wall, and I had a good view of the hockey game on the television. Boston was ahead at the end of the second period by a two-to-one margin over Detroit. I settled in on the stool, and I was satisfied. It was a good seat, with no one sitting on either side of me, and a full view of the game, as well as the rest of the pub. The young gal glanced over her shoulder at me and smiled once more, but I just stared ahead and kept my eyes on the screen.

"What will you have there, longhair?" The barkeeper stood in front of me and he startled me as I had been paying attention to the game. "I would not think a guy like you was into hockey," he chuckled a little at his remark, and he wiped his hands on a towel tucked inside of his belt.

I looked up and smiled. Folks are usually nice around these parts, but tonight a few of these chaps had a bit of an edge to them. I could not help but think how, just a few, short years ago, if my best buddy Harry were with me, a comment such as that one could have set up quite a bit of a ruckus.

However, that was now in my mind, an old life, a moment that passed me in time. Simply a memory.

If only the barkeeper knew what I was into, but instead, I asked him politely, "I do not suppose you serve Big Boulder beer around these parts, do you?"

"Big Boulder, nah, sorry. None of that rot gut around here. With your accent, you must be from New York City. They serve that down that way, in New Jersey, New York, and Connecticut."

"No, sir. I am not from New York City. I am from northern New Jersey. Hey, just pour what is on tap that is local and that you recommend. My old man says that there is really not any bad beer, just those horrible Dingleberries."

"Dingleberry beer, oh man, only had it once. Way too sweet. I will get you a Laconia Pine Street Ale. It is good, not expensive, and produced by a brewery by the big lake in Laconia. It is a small brewery near Paugus Bay on the edge of the lake."

"Sounds good, thanks. Please, pour it in a tall glass if you have them."

He nodded and waved in acknowledgement of my order. I watched the barkeeper pouring the beer out of the tap. He seemed awful young to be a bartender, most of the barkeeps I had run into as of late, were always older, and it seemed funny, but they always had little or no hair. This chap had thick, curly black hair, and I imagined that he could have been of Irish descent. For all I knew, he was a member of the family of owners of the establishment.

He returned and set the ale out in front of me. I had stood up to pull my wallet out of my back pocket and I placed some money down on the bar.

I explained, "I will order some food too, I just need a bit of time to enjoy this ale."

"Whoa! Big guy! You did not look so big seated on the end there." He smiled, waved his hand a little in jest, and said, "I guess that I should have not made that longhair comment."

I sat back down and he took a few dollars off the pile of money. He stopped and placed the dollars back on the pile. He reached out his hand and said, "If you are going to order some food, we can settle up at the end. The name is Kyle. Kyle Murphy."

Now, this was the Concord, New Hampshire, in which I

had become accustomed to on my previous visits!

I took his hand, smiled, and answered, "No offense. I get it all the time. Paul Henson is the name." I squeezed his hand hard, but I did not give him one of my death grips.

"Whoa, boy! Strong guy too." Kyle shook his hand in the air as he asked me, "Say, what brings you to Concord?"

I wanted to avoid any mention of what I did for a living, so I simply said, "Just some traveling business. I spend a lot of time on the road." I shifted gears away from my purposely vague answer.

"Say, in a few minutes, could I please have a plate of the bangers and mash? I had that the last time that I was here back in September and it was very good. It reminded me of my Mum's cooking just a bit."

Kyle Murphy stared at me, and then he wrote the order on his pad. "Sure, no sweat. The bangers are good. You are not Irish though, maybe English, but not Irish. Now, that I look at you, I think I know you. I think you were in here a few months back? Maybe?" Kyle studied my face for a bit, and it seemed as if a memory came to him.

He continued, "I now remember you. I was working the floor that night, but my dad was at the bar. He told me about you when you left. You are a goaltender for the Albany hockey team that is in town today. Big star, too. I read about you in the 'Concord Flyer' sports section. Sure, now I remember . . . a goalie from New Jersey. They had a picture of you in the net, but you could see your hair sticking out from under the mask. That is why you were watching the game." Kyle smiled at me, as he felt that he had worked around my smoke screen after all.

Oh well, the hair gives me away all the time. Folks always seemed to remember a hippie goalie from New Jersey. I took a sip of ale and admitted, "Yeah, yeah, yeah, that is me. I am English, or at least my mother is. A little Welsh too. My old man, well, he is from New Jersey. I speak some Welsh. Do you know any Gaelic?"

"No, I do not. I love that New Jersey yeah, yeah, yeah, stuff, and your accent. It is wonderful. A New Jersey goalie who speaks Welsh and your mum is English. Quite a combination there, Paul. Say, did we win or did your team?"

"We won. Sorry, Kyle. Three to one, but it was a good game."

He nodded and said, "I will get your order in. I will not tell anyone who you are, Paul. I can tell that you fly quietly."

"Thanks. There might be some Concord fans here, and I do not want to start a hockey brawl!"

I went back to watching the game and sipped my ale. The brew was fresh, and it was very good. On a commercial break in the game, I gazed out at the pub floor and studied some faces of the people seated around the floor of the pub.

I wondered what their individual stories were. What were they all thinking, or doing in their lives right now? Were some of them escaping lost loves, as I was trying hard to do? Were some of them seeking adventures and were far from their own homes, but were feeling lost and empty? I know I was, and despite living out my dream of playing professional ice hockey, I still could not shake the terrible, empty feeling inside of me. Were some, despite the crowd in here, and people all around, lonely, feeling slightly lost, while seeking some kind of direction? If I reached deep within me, that was also a description of me, and how I currently felt.

This had been a hard adjustment in the last three months or so, especially for a young man, whom, except for a short stint in Kansas City, Missouri with a hockey club, had never wandered very far from his home. Now, the adventure was there, but parts of me were missing.

It was all very strange.

I imagined that some folks came to watch the Boston

Bears game on the television, but most locals came just out of habit, to have a place of friendly confines to share each other's company and toss a drink or two.

I put my elbow on the bar and tucked my hand under my head. Tonight, was very different, as despite the solid win, and playing a very good game in the net, my mood was melancholy. I could not shake the inner sadness tonight. Perhaps it was the time of the year, the change from the warmth of summer to the colder months. It was as if time ticked on a few notches. But I still was not where I wanted to be.

Past scenes ran through my head, of good times I had with Harry, Rose, and Binky. I could see them now, as I stood in the net, all three of them sitting in a row in the stands watching my hockey game and waving to me. I was smiling under my mask when I spotted them in the crowd, and I waved back to them with my goalie stick. I thought of dates that Binky and I shared as we sat over dinner chatting for hours upon hours. The memories of a warm summer night sitting next to Binky on a park bench for hours, talking about any subject that came into our heads. I could see her hair, her beautiful face, and I could hear her soft voice as she rambled on about her latest efforts researching a long-forgotten subject. I remembered the feel of her soft skin, the glow of her eyes that night, and later on, the unrivaled passion in which we shared. My mind wandered while I wondered where she was right now, what she was doing, and why it all had unraveled as it had. Her memories haunted me and I wondered about all of it, and I had no answers for any of it. I took a long sip of the ale, while thinking that misery loves company, and sometimes, there is nothing like a few sips of some liquid courage, for temporarily enhancing your rather despondent and wandering state of mind.

2

The Stranger

I spotted out of the corner of my eye, the door to the pub open, and inside walked a man. He walked quickly, and he was very large and tall, so he took long strides, and covered ground quickly.

He was dressed all in black, with sharply creased black trousers, a black shirt, and a black leather vest that, despite the cold weather, was unbuttoned except for the last button before his waist. On his head was a black hat with a wide brim which was pulled down close to his ears, but you could still make out some of his facial features, even in the dim lights of the pub.

I could not help but think that although his clothes seemed so expensive and brand new, he appeared as if he was from the past, from some bygone era in time.

Regardless, he was indeed striking in his demeanor and appearance. The man wore a thin, closely trimmed beard that neatly framed his face. On his feet were black, sharp-tipped boots, with a metal clip on the edge that made a distinct clicking noise while he walked along the wooden floor. He walked with an air of confidence as he strode along. You could tell that this was a gentleman that was used to traveling around, and you could easily see that he was comfortable in many types of surroundings.

The man walked over to a coat rack on the side of the pub, removed his hat and vest, and placed them upon a hook on the rack. He then smoothed his hair, tucked in his shirt, and made his way up the center aisle of the pub.

As was the case when I walked in a few minutes earlier, I could guess that this chap was also a stranger, as folks glanced at him and stared his way. Some people nodded, and some even waved, but the stranger did not acknowledge them or even glance their way. He passed the table with the young ladies seated at it, and they all glanced up. One of the ladies pointed at the boots he had on his feet, but they did not speak a word to him. The stranger stopped in front of the bar, looked up and down the bar stools, and then, seeing that there were some open on my end, the stranger walked over towards me.

He looked at me and nodded.

I nodded back.

He then took the seat on the right side next to mine. There remained now, only one open seat left along the entire bar, and that one was between the stranger and the back wall of the pub.

I thought about how this place did some fabulous amount of business; despite the old, worn exterior appearance, it was a gold mine inside!

The second period of the game ended. I leaned back, and finished my ale. It was a good ale; it was not a Big Boulder brand beer around Harry's kitchen table, but not many things in this new life of mine were as enjoyable as that experience was.

I glanced over at the stranger, but I did not say a word. I sensed that he, as I did . . . preferred to be alone. There in the bright light of the bar, you could see that he was about fifty years of age, and with his neatly trimmed, black hair and beard, he was a strikingly handsome man, with piercing brown eyes, which focused dead straight ahead. His weathered face had a few wrinkles around his eyes and along the side of his face.

Kyle came over with his towel and a glass coaster and said, "Hello" to the stranger as he placed the coaster in front of him. The stranger still said not a word, but simply nodded his head just a little in the direction of Kyle Murphy. Kyle took his towel and wiped down the top of the bar in front of the stranger next to me.

He picked up my mug, wiped the counter and said, "Did you like the ale, Paul? Do you want another?"

"Yeah, yeah, yeah, Kyle, it was good. Please, pour me another. Thank you."

"Sure thing. Your food will be out shortly, Paul."

Kyle then turned towards the stranger and he asked him, "What can I get you to drink or eat, sir? Welcome to Murphy's Pub. What brings you in here tonight? I have never seen you in here before."

The stranger looked back at Kyle and answered with a deep, melodious voice, "Please, a glass of your best, top shelf Scotch with ice, and just a little splash of water." He did not answer Kyle's other question. He reached in his vest pocket, took out a fifty-dollar bill, and laid it down in front of him. Kyle looked at him and then at the money.

"Top shelf, eh? The best we have is going to be a twelve-dollar drink."

The stranger looked at Kyle and did not say a word, he just pointed to the fifty-dollar bill. Kyle nodded and went to prepare the drink.

I thought about how the way this guy next to me was dressed, with the fancy clothes and expensive boots; it was easy to see that spending money was not an issue for him. Kyle came back with the drink, placed it on the coaster, and took the cash. He rang up the drink sale at the register and returned with the change.

"There you go," he said as he laid the cash in front of the stranger, who was now slowly sipping his drink while staring straight ahead. The stranger did not acknowledge Kyle, nor did he engage in any additional conversation at all with him or me. I had pegged him correctly. He just wanted to drink and be alone.

That was fine with me.

Kyle brought out my food and placed it in front of me. "Looks good, Paul, piping hot, too. Be careful. Do you need anything else?"

"No, I am good. It does look good. Thank you."

"You're welcome."

I dug in because I was suddenly very hungry. I was not disappointed. It was fantastic. This pub sure was a hidden gem because the food was spectacular. It tasted as if it were a home cooked meal from back home in my dear Mum's kitchen. Oh boy, how I missed some Shepherd's Pie cooked by Mum on a cold day.

The hockey game had returned for the third and final period. The game was still close; therefore, I was eating and keeping my eyes intently on the screen. A few other folks in the pub were also watching. They gave out shouts when the Boston Bears goaltender made some key saves, and when the team from Detroit rallied, they booed terribly. All in all, they were well behaved, and not a raucous bunch of hockey fans at all. Believe me, coming from the leagues that I had played in earlier in my career, and playing in some rinks of which I played in now, I knew raucous hockey fans!

A middle-aged man caught my eyes as he walked up to the bar. He too, must have just come in the front door, then noticed how crowded the pub was, and headed for the bar. He was wavering just a bit, so I immediately got the impression that he was half in the bag already. His eyes were red, his nose was a little puffy, and he had the look of a hard-core drinker.

As he walked by me, I nodded slightly, while he stopped and looked at me to see if he recognized or knew me. Even in a little drunken haze, he realized that I was a stranger; he glanced back and gave me just a slight acknowledgement with a tip of his head. He stopped, looked up at the score of the game, pulled out the last seat left at the bar, and sat down next to the stranger. His clothes were all in disarray, he had some stubble growth on his face from about a two or three-day beard, and his hair was all messy on top of his head.

He turned and looked at the stranger next to him and said, "How ya doing tonight? The Bears are winning . . . I see."

I then determined that he was a regular patron of the pub, as he progressed to the next step with the questions that every single outsider could count upon having a regular ask him or her around here. He looked long and hard at the stranger next to him, and even through slightly drunken eyes, he knew that he was new in town.

The next words out of his mouth were, of course, "Where are you from? What brings you here? I have never seen you in here before."

The stranger did not react. In fact, he did not even move his eyes, which were locked dead ahead. He just raised his glass and took a sip of Scotch.

"What will you have? How about a Mill Pond Ale, there, Mike?" Kyle had wandered over and it was obvious that my supposition of the situation was correct, as Kyle knew this chap. He was a regular, in fact, from the look on his face; he was a very frequent, regular patron.

"Sure Kyle, hey give me a chaser of rye, too, will you?"

"You have cash right, Mike?"

"Ah sure, sure, sorry about that last night, Kyle, here . . . here." The middle-aged man reached into his pocket, took out a pile of rumpled and crumpled dollar bills, and placed them on the bar. He looked over at the stranger sitting next to him, tapped his shirt pocket, and pulled out a pack of cigarettes. His hands shook and trembled as he removed one cigarette from the pack and pulled a book of matches from the same pocket. He grabbed an ashtray sitting in the corner of the bar top and pulled it in front of him.

"Ya mind?" He asked the stranger as he placed the cigarette in his mouth and allowed it to dangle from his lips.

The stranger never answered him. He continued to stare straight ahead.

The middle-aged man assumed that the stranger did not mind. He shrugged his shoulders, and struggled to light the cigarette. His hands trembled and shook. It was difficult to determine if his tremors were alcohol related, or just his nerves. He finally lit the cigarette, took a long drag, and blew the smoke away from us up towards the rear of the bar.

This guy was a mess.

He looked at Kyle and told him, "Take what I stiffed you for yesterday, out of there too."

Kyle nodded, looked at the stranger, saw that he was still working on his drink, and then he checked on me.

"It was good, right? You did not leave a morsel on your plate there, Paul."

"Great, really good. I will have another ale too, Kyle. Thanks."

"Sure thing," Kyle said as he took my plate and mug.

Kyle returned with my drink, as well as the ale and rye whiskey for the man at the end of the bar. The middle-aged man first hurled the shot of rye whiskey down his gullet, tipping his head back. And in an instant, it was gone. Then he moved to the ale, and it did not take him very long to empty his mug of Pine Street's best brew. He downed it about as quickly as I had ever seen anyone drink alcohol. In a flash, he was waving Kyle back over for a refill.

This middle-aged man had some serious issues. I began to feel sorry for him, and I wondered what his story was. I watched him out of the corner of my eye, but no one in our small circle said anything. The stranger just sipped his drink and hardly moved a muscle.

The Bears scored two quick, back-to-back goals and it looked as though they had this game in the bag. All they needed to do was to protect the puck in their own zone, play keep away for five minutes, and this game was over. The locals were happy, and some loud claps filtered through the pub here and there, after the Bears scored the last goal to put the game in the bag. I smiled, as this was hockey country. I felt right at home. Well, in certain ways, I did.

In the short time that it took for the Boston Bears to score a few goals and ice the game, the middle-aged man had gone through even more ales and another shot. I was sure that he was pretty well lit up by now.

When he waved Kyle over for another ale, Kyle asked him, "You are walking right, Mike?"

"Oh sure, Kyle. I do not have a car. My wife still has it. I have not been able to get it back. Now, she will not even answer my phone calls." He snuffed out another cigarette in the ashtray in front of him.

The picture now became a lot clearer. He was drowning his sorrows and numbing himself from the pain. When he had finished the sentence, his eyes went down to the bar, and I saw a level of intense sadness come over him. The drinks had numbed him, but the reality had not left.

His mouth quivered, and his eyes rolled back in his head a little. He had some tears forming in the corners of his eyes, which he pushed away with his hands. He had revealed the source of his pain; which Kyle must have known some of beforehand.

The beer and whiskey must have now been taking full effect, and for some reason, the middle-aged man felt compelled to convey aloud to the stranger all the pain that he was feeling. He turned to the stranger and said, "You know, I just don't know what to do anymore."

The stranger did not move his body, but his eyes moved slightly towards the middle-aged man, and then back to his drink in front of him when the middle-aged man had finished speaking the sentence.

"I cannot find a job, no matter how hard I try. I just can't get it together."

The hockey game ended, and some cheers went up throughout the bar. I even clapped a little; after all, the Bears were in a roundabout way responsible for my paycheck!

Suddenly, the middle-aged man had the words pouring out of him. Whether it was the drink that had loosened his lips, or his own emotions, I could not tell, but for some reason, he felt the need to continue to speak. Even from one seat away, I could hear the conversation clearly. The middle-aged man was speaking directly to the stranger and not to me, but I leaned my head over and listened as I kept my other eye and ear on the wrap-up of the hockey game. I had to admit, I was more than just a bit curious as to what his story was.

"It has been so hard. My wife just would not understand. She just kept yelling and putting more and more pressure on me to find a better job, do something with my life, go make more money. Everything that went wrong was always my fault. I got the blame for everything. No job was ever good enough for her, it was never enough money, and nothing ever worked, or made her happy. It was always something with her. The kids needed clothes. They needed shoes, and toys and this and that. The bills were piling up, and I just could not get through to her about how much pain I was in these days. She just would not help me. She would not even try to understand. One day, a week or so ago, I just took off. I could not take it anymore, and I left."

The middle-aged man picked up his mug and held it in his hand, but did not drink from it, but instead continued to speak to the stranger.

His hand, which was holding the mug, trembled, and I could see the ale moving about in the mug as he spoke, "Now, I feel I should not have left, it was a big mistake, but it eased my pain for a few short days, it was as if I was somehow, set free. I love my wife, despite how she treats me, and what she says to me, and I love my children. It is as if a part of me feels relieved, but my wife tore the other part of me in two. Now, I cannot tell you how lonely I am, and the pain of this loneliness is like nothing that I have ever felt before."

With that, the stranger who up to this point had not said a word or even moved gently shook his head back and forth a little. It seemed that when the middle-aged man had said the word, "lonely," it had sparked something within the stranger. It was apparent that the quiet stranger was now sitting there thinking, almost pondering the word in his mind.

The stranger turned to the middle-aged man, and he finally spoke, "There is actually no loneliness in this world. You will not be lonely, as long as you realize that God or a single person out there in the world cares for you." The stranger's eyes turned towards the ale being held by the man and he continued to speak, "You should have found strength and guidance in your pain, but instead, you are trying to find an answer in the bottom of that mug, but the answer is not there, the answer is in your heart. The loneliness will leave you—once you follow your heart and do what you already know is right." The stranger then turned back to his drink, picked it up, took a sip of it, and he said no more.

Kyle came over and spoke to the stranger, "Would you like another drink, sir?" The stranger did not answer. He simply tapped the money on the bar top and nodded his head.

"I will get it for you," Kyle responded.

The comments from the stranger astounded me, and I could tell that the comments had astounded the middle-aged man too. They had struck a chord in both of us. I had felt the same pain since I had left home, and Binky had left me. I knew very well the feelings of loneliness, which the middle-aged man now felt from leaving his wife and children. It was obvious that he loved his wife and his family, and in utter despair, he had made a bad choice. He had made a knee jerk reaction, instead of doing what the stranger had said, "In following his heart and doing what he already knew was right."

I felt some comfort that I was not actually alone. My religious beliefs were always strong. I knew God, and felt God's presence in my life, but it was something that I very much kept to myself. It was a comfort to know that my beliefs were there for me to lean upon during these days, and I should never forget that. Being on the road now, playing hockey, left little time for attending church or worship services. The team had a team chaplain assigned to us, and I made a mental note to contact him when we arrived back in Albany.

In the hustle and bustle of my new life, perhaps, I too had felt sorry for myself, just a little too much. I had more than just hockey to keep my mind off Binky. I had God, loving friends, and family to turn to these days, and it had been very easy to forget that until now.

This was a timely reminder, and it eased some of my own pain.

The middle-aged man wanted to speak, and he almost started his reply a few times, but the words stalled and they would not come out. I could tell that he badly wanted to have a rebuttal for the stranger, but it seemed as though his mind was blank, and the words would not formulate in his alcohol-altered state of mind.

He looked down at his own appearance; his eyes scanned his messy clothes. He then reached his hand up to the top of his head to feel his messy hair. He rubbed his unshaven face, and then he glanced at his clothes once again. Once more, he looked over at the stranger sitting there. The stranger was shiny, clean, and neat as a pin, all decked out in perfectly tailored clothes that cost more than a person could ever imagine.

Somewhere along the line, it was obvious that the stranger had solved some of these same troubles in his own life. Perhaps, he had confronted some demons along the way, and he had won the battles that all men face at sometime in their lives.

Kyle came over, set the new drink for the stranger, and looked over to the middle-aged man. The middle-aged man took some dollar bills from out of his pocket and laid them across the bar in the direction of Kyle. Kyle did not say a word, but he shrugged his shoulders. I think Kyle was surprised that he was leaving so soon and not ordering another drink.

The middle-aged man did not say another word. He jumped off the bar stool, steadied himself when he landed, and took off towards the center aisle of the pub. He waved to one or two of the locals and hustled up the aisle towards the front of the pub. I watched as he went over to the coat hooks. He searched amongst the clothing for his coat and hat, found them, and put them on. The middle-aged man then turned and looked our way once more. I noticed his face broke out into just the slightest smile. He opened the door and stepped out into the cold night air, and he was gone.

Somehow, someway, in this little exchange, I think he found some answers that he may have been looking for, or perhaps he just woke up. I knew that I did, and I found myself fascinated by the curious stranger and his unique but purposeful behavior.

It was almost as if he had planned it, as though he knew what the man was going to ask him ahead of time.

The stranger picked up his refill and slowly sipped it. But still, his eyes stayed almost straight ahead, and he did not say a single word.

The game wrapped up now and the television station had switched over to a late-night news broadcast. Kyle came over to check on us. I tilted back my mug and finished off the rest of the ale.

"Are you finished, Paul?"

"Yes. Thanks, Kyle. Would you happen to have some tea that you could brew? I could go for a cup to cap off the night."

"Of course, it is not only you Englishmen who enjoy your tea. I will brew a cup for you. Cream and sugar?"

"Just cream. Thanks."

I was very tempted to say, at least, "Hello" to the man next to me, but I resisted. I was going to respect his space and his wish to be alone. For some strange reason, deep inside, I felt that if he wanted to say something to me—then he would.

My eyes scanned the pub floor, and the crowd had thinned just a bit now that the game had ended. I spotted some musicians now gathering around the stage. They were having a few beers and setting up some more instruments. I looked at my watch and saw that it was about nine thirty or so. I was sure that they would begin to play music, around ten o'clock or so, for the late-night crowd. It looked as if from the type of instruments, they had set about, as though they might be an Irish folk band. As much as I enjoyed music, I was not going to stick around for the performance. The team had a midnight curfew on the road for a Saturday night, so I would just finish the tea and head on back to the hotel. I was getting a little tired. We had left Albany early in the morning, and the game was a tough one.

The pretty, young gal from the table close to the bar glanced my way once or twice and our eyes met, but I carefully avoided any projection of any interest in meeting her acquaintance. I did notice, however, a middle-aged lady sitting alone at a table that was one table over from where the young gals were sitting. She had also just finished her meal and now had a full glass of red wine in front of her. I would have guessed her to be in her middle to late forties, and she was one of those types of ladies that you would say was not unattractive, but she was not a ravishing bombshell. She had her own style, and in her own way, she was indeed quite beautiful.

She was well dressed, in a tight black dress with a low-cut neckline. Her hair was short and neatly prepared. She was eyeing the open seat next to the stranger. By following her eyes, I now guessed that she had watched the seat become vacant after the middle-aged man had left, and she was going to try her luck with the handsome stranger. I surmised that she had undoubtedly been watching the stranger since the moment that he walked into the pub. I guess years of watching shooter's eyes in ice hockey to determine their next move had carried over to my "civilian" life.

Sure enough, she picked up her wine, and she slowly made her way to the end of the bar. She signaled her server to carry over her tab.

She then steadied the wine glass in her hand, sauntered over to the bar, grabbed the seat next to the stranger, turned, and asked, "Is this seat being saved for someone? Do you mind if I sit here?"

I could tell by her reaction when she spoke to the stranger and when she saw him up close that he fascinated her with his handsome appearance. She smiled broadly, adjusted her hair, and tugged at her dress just a bit to reveal a touch more of her cleavage. She was clearly thrilled at the empty seat next to the stranger, and the opportunity to engage in a potentially rewarding conversation with him.

This was turning out to be a fascinating evening for me as I studied these interactions from my adjoining bar stool.

The stranger did not answer her, but only slightly nodded and it was hard to say whether he had actually meant yes or no. Predictably, the woman took that to be an approval. She took the seat and immediately tried to start up with a conversation. It was easy to see that she was a gregarious and outgoing person. She had a wonderful smile and a joyful approach.

She even leaned over and around the stranger and said, "Hello there" to me.

I returned her greeting with a welcome and a smile.

This was going to be a good one! A chatterbox next to Mr. Solitude. I remained anxious to see how this scene would unfold.

Kyle brought my tea over. I thanked him and asked him for my check. He leaned close to me as if to make sure that no one else heard what he was going to say, "You know Paul, for a long-haired guy, and a professional ice hockey goalie, you are an awfully polite man."

I smiled and said, "I guess that I do not fit the stereotype. Maybe, I should be doing something else with my life, eh?"

I spotted out of the corner of my eye that the stranger had moved his head slightly; he must have picked up what Kyle had said, despite his lowered voice. I wondered if my profession surprised him or not.

The woman at the end of the bar now jumped in, as she had decided to make her move. Hey, I guess you cannot blame a gal for trying! Being talkative by nature, she picked up with some same lines that Kyle and the middle-aged man had tried, with no success, earlier.

"Where are you from? What brings you here? I have never seen you in here before," and so on and so forth, she went on and on, as she worked hard in an attempt to start a conversation with the stranger.

To her frustration, he would not answer her, and he said not one word. He just sat there, sipping his drink and staring at the back of the bar. Once or twice, he moved his eyes up to the television screen as if he was vaguely interested in what the program might be that came on after the hockey game had ended.

For the most part, though, the stranger was eerily silent.

I had to admire her efforts because the woman did not give up easily. She continued with general attempts at conversation. She tried some comments about the crowd in the pub this evening, how cold it was getting outside, how the game had ended in Boston's favor, and other chitchat. No matter what the chatterbox said, she realized that she was not going to crack what seemed to be an iron fortress of silence around this stranger.

Kyle walked over and asked her if she would like some more red wine.

She thanked him and said, "Yes, just one more glass please, Kyle."

Kyle looked at the stranger and pointed to his glass. He seemed to know by now that the chap was not going to answer, so a simple gesture would suffice for communication. The stranger put up one finger to signal that he was going to have one more. Kyle was off to fill the orders.

I sipped my tea slowly. It was an excellent tea, very well brewed, but it was really hot. I needed to let it cool a bit, or just sip it carefully as not to cook the inside of my mouth.

I could see by the look on the woman's face that she had conceded defeat, and that she now had some growing sadness inside of her. She realized that this conversation was going to go nowhere. She became quieter and more than a little disconcerted.

Kyle came over, placed another red wine down for her, wiped the bar with his rag, dropped the drink for the stranger, and handed me my check. I stood back up off the stool, and I saw the stranger's eyes follow me from the floor to the top of my head. Perhaps he, too, had not realized how tall I was. I took my wallet out and counted out some additional money to pay my check.

The woman took her purse, opened it, and put a few

dollars on the bar. It looked as though she was going to finish her wine and then call it a night. I am sure she felt that she had tried, but she had struck out on this one. Her face and eyes had lost the excitement and the joy that she originally had just a few short minutes ago. I could not help but see some pain and some sadness there. In fact, it was just a little hard to tell, but I thought I could see some tears forming in the corners of her eyes. I think this little failure was somehow the culmination of a situation, the pinnacle of emotions that had led the woman to this point in time.

The woman closed her purse up and she took a longer sip of wine. I could tell that she was trying to finish it to get ready to leave, when both to my utter shock, and the woman's surprise, suddenly, the stranger turned to her and asked, "What kind of wine are you drinking?"

It caught her by surprise—as it did me too!

The stranger had ignored all the previous questions that she had asked, all the words, in which she had previously spoken, had been a futile attempt at inducing a response from the stranger, and now, out of nowhere, he suddenly has asked her what appeared to be a very simple question!

"Oh, oh," her response was clearly flustered, "it is red merlot. I really like the merlot wines, and I enjoy this one. I drink it whenever I come in here."

A glimmer of hope came over her, and it was very obvious to see that her confidence returned. She felt the need to smile broadly at the stranger. It appeared, as if for a second or two, the sadness that was in her eyes might be leaving.

The stranger did not smile back, or say anything. He just looked at her and then at her wine

glass. I watched as the woman's facial expression went flat, and her face changed from a broad smile to a serious look. Perhaps, it was the drink. I had no idea how much wine she had consumed before she joined us at the bar, but she seemed sober to me and spoke clearly. Once more, it was very strange, but not unlike the man before her. The woman also was suddenly compelled to divulge what she was feeling in her heart to this stranger in black. A man she did not even know, but for some reason, she had no concern at all about pouring out her innermost feelings.

"You know, I just have to get out of this old city. I really feel that I need to leave here." So, it began, she turned on her story; she mysteriously poured out of her innermost soul, about her dreams of traveling the world, how long she has been stuck here in Concord, New Hampshire, how boring and horrible it was, and so on and so forth, she carried on with her long list of laments and complaints.

I sipped my tea and waited. This was certainly a most unusual hour or two that I had spent here tonight.

The stranger just listened, and stared at her with his deep set, dark eyes, carefully watching the woman pour out her inner ambitions and dreams, but never saying a word. On and on she went for about five minutes, in a long monologue of a magnificent outpouring of emotional pain, until she ran out of words. Then she stopped as she caught herself, more than just a little embarrassed at her actions and chatterbox ways. She realized that once more she had gone on way too long, and perhaps looked a little foolish to the stranger, by revealing so much of what seemed like her silly dreams of travel and ambitions for no real reason at all.

After all, he had only asked her about her wine, not for her life story! She stopped speaking after she realized that the stranger had not said another word.

She and I both watched him take a long sip of his Scotch. I could tell that this man of very few words was about to say something.

He looked back at the woman and the stranger said, "I have traveled around, in fact, I have been all over this world, and what feels like a few others, I can tell you for certain that there is no, Isle of Avalon. Sometimes, what seems like such a wonderful place to be or to visit is not so wonderful at all. Once the glimmer wears off and shine is gone, you realize that in the end, there are many more people that love and care for you at home, and there are a lot of reasons to stay right where you are. You learn that it is a lot better to be with people who love and care about you, and with what you are comfortable with, then to be uncomfortable in some far off, strange place, chasing some silly dream."

The words he spoke shook me to my very inner being and soul. They tore at me and twisted my insides like a vise. I knew in my heart that my dear Binky had left me and done exactly that. She went off chasing a dream when there were so many people who loved and cared about her at home.

Moreover, I was one of them.

The woman listened, and when the stranger had finished speaking of his experience, she smiled at him. His words seemed as if they were a profound, personal testimony. They were so authoritative and resounding; I could tell that the words had struck a chord deep inside of her, too.

The stranger returned to staring straight ahead, and he spoke no more. It was as if he was looking way past the confines of the bar. Perhaps he was dreaming of a far-off place that he had traveled to a long time ago, or maybe he was dreaming of his home wherever that may have been. It seemed as though, somehow, or someway that he had given the woman a special answer. I suspected it was an answer, which she had been somehow searching for a very long time to find. It also seemed that he had given to her the solution as to why she dreamt all the time, but deep inside, she knew the real reason that she never acted upon those dreams and ambitions.

I watched as she reached in her purse. Her face was

different. She was confident, reassured, and radiant.

She was now an even more beautiful woman, because she shined from the inside as well as the outside.

She placed some more money on the bar and waved to Kyle. She slid out of the bar stool and whispered, "Goodbye and thank you," to the stranger, but the words were barely audible. She nodded and smiled at me as she passed, and I returned the same. She turned and went to the side of the pub wall directly behind us.

There was a pay telephone hanging on the wall, just a few feet away from us. The woman took out some coins from her purse and she dropped them in the slot for the phone. Her hands were shaking as she dialed the number on the old, rotary telephone. I could hear the clicks of the telephone as the dial spun behind me.

I tried not to be obvious, but my curiosity, as well as some other folks in and around the telephone, could not help but watch as the scene unfolded a few feet away from us.

The stranger, however, did not move, but he did take a long, final sip of his drink and placed his glass back on the bar top.

You could overhear that she was speaking to herself as the phone was ringing, as she said aloud, "Please, please, answer the phone," she was repeating over and over. The person on the other end, did apparently answer the phone, and she shouted a loud, "Oh, hello!" She was now unable to conceal her joy when the person had finally answered. You could hear that the two of them had started a conversation, and that her voice was now emotional and excited.

"You know that I have been so stupid, so pigheaded. I now realize that there is no Isle of Avalon. There are no glorious apple trees or grape vineyards that miraculously grow without care or needs, there are no golden bridges, or shiny roads in faraway places. I think I clearly know that you have to go where your heart leads you. I now know that I just want to stay here, and I want to be with you. Is it too late? Can I come over? Can we talk?"

The woman was almost crying into the phone now.

Whoever it was that was on the other end of the line must have told her to come, and to come over quickly, because the woman thanked the person over and over. She explained that she was on her way and ended the conversation with a loud and emphatic, "I love you!"

She hung up the phone and with a smile on her face, she ran up the center aisle of the pub, went to the coat rack, grabbed her coat as quickly as she could, and ran out the front door.

3

Five Leaves

Once more, I have to say that this was certainly one of the strangest few hours that I had experienced in a very long time. I was used to strange and wild encounters in my life, and I had to admit ever since I had met my best buddy's wife, Sky Blu Redmond, I had noticed that I seemed to be tuned into certain unusual aspects of life, which seemed even more peculiar than I had ever noticed before.

Kyle came over, and I gave him the cash for the dinner check. I reached over the bar and shook his hand gently. Kyle then looked at the stranger. The man dressed all in black had slid off the bar stool, pointed at the remaining cash on the bar, and then back to Kyle. He then turned and started to walk away. I heard the click of the metal tips of his boots on the floor as he moved away.

"Hey, thanks for everything, Kyle. I think we will be back in Concord, right after Thanksgiving for another game, so I will be sure to stop in and say hello. I hope I can bring my best buddy on the team, Rick Tremblay next time. He would have come tonight, but he had girlfriend issues."

"Nice to see you, Paul. I will look forward to your next trip into Concord. Say . . . ah . . . that strange guy next to you sure did not say much."

"No, but what he said, sure meant a lot."

I am sure that Kyle did not understand, but he slipped a little piece of paper and a pen to me and smiled, then asked, "Do you mind? In case, you make it to the big league."

"Sure, no sweat." I signed it for him, put number twenty-seven under it, and handed it back to him.

"Hey, thank you there, number twenty-seven. Good luck this year, except when you play the Concord team!"

I waved to him and I was off.

I was walking behind the stranger as we both made our way up the center aisle. As I passed the table with the young ladies, the pretty gal on the end slid out of her chair and stood up in front of me.

She had obviously been waiting for this moment. She smiled as I stopped in front of her in the center aisle. The gal was fairly short and I towered over her. I surmised that she was finally going to make her move.

"Hi there, number twenty-seven, goalie guy. We were at the game today. I knew it was you right away when you walked in. You are an unreal goalie. You shut us down today."

I just smiled and said, "Thanks."

"Handsome, professional, ice hockey goalies, with long hair and beards do not come by here very often. Please call me next time that you are in Concord." She grabbed my hand and placed in my palm, a paper that I am sure had her contact information on it.

I placed the paper in my pocket.

I did smile and as I passed her, I simply added, "Have a nice evening."

I followed behind the stranger who now was almost to the front of the pub when I saw him slip around a table that had about ten or so young men sitting around it. One of the young men was sitting at the end of the table because it was so full; therefore, he was actually sitting out in the middle of the center aisle.

When the stranger passed, he bumped his leg a little on the side of the chair where the young man was sitting. The young man on the end seemed to be loud and more than just a little drunk, and he also seemed as though he was a show off, or the "ringleader" of the rest of the group that was seated there. When he felt the accidental bump, the young man dramatically sprung out of his chair and jumped in front of the stranger.

Oh boy, this could turn bad very quickly. This was not anything that I want to be involved with or be in between. My hockey sense knew when it was going to turn bad very quickly, and I steered clear of these sorts of situations. I could more than handle myself in a little fist-a-cuffs both on the ice and off. I was big, tall, and strong, and even though I was a goalie, I had grown up on the gritty streets of Paterson, and I could tussle with anyone and usually come out ahead.

People who knew me back home as well as on the ice knew that it took a long time to anger me, but you had better steer clear when I did finally crack, because it was not very pretty. Goalies are used to stitches, cuts, and missing teeth, so if you tangle with one, you had better bring your best game, or you are going to lose!

When I was younger, and a lot dumber, and over our many years together, Harry and I had fought our way out of many bars and situations on the ice, and off, but I made a point now of staying out of trouble, away from too much drink, and any wild ladies. I had a professional career at stake, so I just stood there for a minute.

I intended to stay far away from this one.

The ringleader blocked off the main walkway, and he stood there with a stupid, alcohol-induced smirk on his face. His buddies all started to laugh in anticipation of having a little fun with this sharply dressed stranger.

Some patrons in the pub turned to watch as they saw what was going on and wondered what shenanigans this group of want-to-be hooligans was going to try next. I could easily detect that although they thought that they were tough guys; they had no real idea of what tough really was.

The stranger stopped a few feet away from the ringleader; he just stared at him with his piercing dark eyes, and suddenly the ringleader's false bravado faded a little at the sight of the stranger close up. He realized that the stranger was a very large man, in fact, he was immense, and the stranger displayed no fear at all about the situation that the ringleader had foolishly decided to attempt here.

I could tell. I dealt all the time with intimidation, and the testing of men's courage in hockey. It was very plain to see that the stranger had been in a few of these types of confrontations in his past. Turning and running scared was not an option or something that he would do in these types of situations.

Even through his drunken haze, the ringleader knew that he had made a miscalculation in his little attempt to show off for his buddies. The rest of the young men grew quiet at the table as they also realized that the stranger was not the type of man that you tried to provoke or falsely incite.

Now caught, the ringleader looked for an easy way out of his little adventure, without adversely affecting his artificial image as a tough guy. He stammered and tried his best not to look like too much of a fool in front of his drinking pals. Deep in his mind, the sight of this large, tall stranger had invoked true fear in his heart, and he really did not know what to say.

Embarrassed, drunk, and now finding it difficult to stand, he stumbled at his words. And he said the first thing that popped into his intoxicated mind.

He slurred out, "Oh sir, excuse me. I did not see you walking up the aisle. I did not know what direction you were going to go."

I was happy to see that the young man had made a solid choice and not allowed his drunken state of mind to lead him down the wrong path this evening. I sensed a much calmer situation, so I walked up behind the stranger. The stranger looked at the young man for what seemed as if it was a long time. I watched as the stranger's eyes went back and forth from the young man to the table where his buddies all sat.

The stranger said in a low voice, just above a whisper, "Sometimes, the direction you think you are going is not really where you will end up."

When he heard those words, the young ringleader moved out of the aisle, and sunk back down in his chair at the table; he just strangely and abruptly collapsed down into the confines of the chair.

The stranger walked past the table of the young men and strode quickly to the coat rack where he put on his vest and hat and moved to the front door.

I thought how that was such a strange reaction for the young man to have made and wondered where the ringleader was in his life that such a short sentence had made such a profound impact upon him. It was as though those words meant so much more than just a simple statement in reference to walking around someone.

I looked once more at the table with the young man sitting there, and then I walked to the front door. The stranger had opened the door and the cold air rushed into the warm pub. He turned and looked at me. He did not say a word, but he did hold the door open for me.

I said, "Thank you," and stepped up my pace. We both stepped outside and went down the odd-sized front step together. I stood next to him now in the cold darkness. He was tall, but not quite as tall as I was. He adjusted his hat on top of his head, turned to me, and placed his hand upon my shoulder.

I felt a cold chill go down my spine as I looked at him.

"Those words were meant for you too, my long-haired friend."

He then warmly smiled. I could see, even in the dim

reflected light of the pub, a twinkle in his dark eyes. He then spun around to walk away, gave me a little head nod, a tip of his hat, and then a slight wave of his hand.

I stood and watched as he walked briskly away.

I stood there for a long time, pondering his words, and all that had happened during these very strange few hours.

My mind searched my past, and I remembered the words that Sky Blu Redmond had told me on the night when I first met her, "You are very spiritual, you believe in God, and what is right and kind. There is an inner light and fire inside of you Paul, you can feel it, and others can sense it. You would make a great religious leader."

I wondered once more who that man was and why we had met. The fact that this was All Saint's Day made this all so much the stranger. I could hear his boots clicking upon the cold sidewalk as he walked farther away from me. For some reason, I still could not move. I just stood there, watching and listening.

The darkness of this autumn evening was now complete blackness, with only a few street lamps glowing here and there to interrupt the darkness. The clouds now covered up the previous moonlight. An intense cold filled the night air. The kind of cold that would really be more like a winter's night, rather than just an autumn prelude.

The sharp click of the metal tips of the stranger's boots echoed as he walked farther and farther away from the pub. The sounds slowly faded away in the distance . . . until I could no longer hear them.

I looked up when I heard the old metal sign above the front door of the pub squeaking a tune as it waved in the wind. Back and forth the sign swayed, crying for oil to put it out of its misery.

Reaching down into my pocket, I pulled out the little piece of paper with the young lady's information written on it. I glanced at the young lady's name and telephone number scrawled upon it. Who knows, she might just be a wonderful gal. She seemed pleasant, well spoken, and very pretty. She also was a hockey fan!

For some reason, I had also remembered Sky Blu telling me, "People never really go away forever. Even when they die, they return to us, somehow. We remain together forever with the people that we love. She will return to you someday, I can tell."

My voice was just a whisper, "I surely hope so Sky, I surely hope so."

I took the little piece of paper and tore it into the smallest little pieces that I possibly could and I held them up into the wind.

The wind caught the pieces, and then scattered them for all time, while I watched and smiled. Satisfied, I made my way towards the main street and the hotel.

The pile of leaves that had been dancing around on the street in front of the pub continued to follow one another around. The noises that they made as the wind chased them were a sad reminder of their past glory as now, they were simply dried reminders of spring and summer spent wonder. A strong gust of wind blew down the sidewalk while I started to walk up the side street. I looked at my watch and saw that it was just past ten now.

There was plenty of time.

I pulled my old trusty vest up around me as the wind was really whistling now. I watched the piles of leaves, as up and down the road they went, rolling over one another, in between parked cars, and into dark corners of the buildings.

The wind blew strongly, and it actually forced me to bow my head down and face the gust, to prevent debris and dried leaves from the pile from getting into my eyes. When the gust had ended, I stared into the darkness and watched the pile of leaves land right in front of me.

Five of the leaves blew out of the pile, straight up into the air they went, higher and higher, they tumbled over one another, until the momentum was lost, and they slowly drifted back down to the ground, fell in amongst the pile, and mixed in with the rest of the leaves.

4

A Different Direction

About four years after I retired from my career in professional ice hockey, I sat rather nervously in a chair within an administrative office of a Lutheran Seminary in New York City. I carefully studied the eyes of the woman sitting on the other side of the desk while she reviewed my application to attend this institution of higher learning.

Deep down within me I was, and will always be, a goaltender. I always study the shooter's eyes for a clue of which direction and location they were planning to shoot the hockey puck.

The woman was now studying an application packet, which contained my resume, an essay on why I wanted to attend seminary, my educational transcripts, letters of recommendation, for the most part, documentation of what was my entire life until this point.

It was a bit hard to read this situation; the administrator would not put her head up in order for me to see where her eyes were leading me.

I sat in silence with my necktie choking me. Finally, she lifted her eyes, held the paper in which she was reading in her right hand and waved it a bit. I recognized the paper as being the front page of my resume.

Finally, the woman rather abruptly spoke, "You really are a retired professional ice hockey goalie? Wow! I must say, this is sure to be a different career path for you to wander down. It all seems strange and unusual for you to enter the Lutheran ministry. All that long hair, and a beard and playing ice hockey, my goodness. Talk about a change of direction."

As soon as she spoke those words, all the anxiety within me melted away.

I recalled a strange night in Concord, New Hampshire, and an old pub, some leaves blowing in the air . . . spent autumn leaves that were all around me, in the dark chill of the evening air.

I also remembered the words of the quiet stranger in the black hat.

It all became so clear to me now.

All the mysteries of life, in which we never will understand or even try to comprehend, but guide us, lead us, and shape what we are, who we love, and the people that we need to touch along the way, all became so much clearer to me.

Life is a long journey.

I thought in my mind, how I left behind a life that meant so much to me, and perhaps, this new life would be a replacement in my heart for the exhilaration that I felt when I was on the ice, in the net, staring down opponents. The sweat dripping off the end of my mask, the sound of a skate cutting an edge on the hard ice, the roar of the crowd, the individual challenge . . . me alone, watching the eyes of the shooters.

I knew that what I missed the most in my heart was that individual challenge.

The mission.

Perhaps I was wrong, and this was all a wild dream. I would be a flop, a failure, and I would have to pick myself back up once again and find another direction to take my life in once more. Despite my unusual background and the overall craziness of presenting my application for her consideration, I knew it was the correct thing to do. For some reason, I no longer had a single doubt harbored within my mind. I knew that I was going to answer my heart and give this crazy idea my best shot.

When life boils down to the final moments, if you can look back and say that you were happy, then you will never have any regrets. The only person that truly knows that you are happy is the person whom you see in the mirror every single day. That person is the one person who is impossible to fool.

I sat back, smiled at her doubts and with quite the air of confidence replied, "Sometimes, the direction you think you are going is not really where you will end up."

THE END

Forever Pensive

She sat upon the park bench in a lonely corner of the city park. She sat in a haven, a safe port in the storm, in a spot where she felt no one, other than an occasional jogger, or dog walker, or another passerby, would notice her.

She had purposely picked this spot. Out of all the hundreds, maybe even thousands, of benches in this park, this one was her bench.

She liked it that way.

Most people thought of her as outgoing, warm, friendly. She was pretty—no, in fact, many people described her as beautiful. She did enjoy socializing; she loved her family, her friends, she admitted that she had all the traits in which folks would describe her as possessing, but there was one word, in which no one except her used to describe her.

Pensive.

Pensive was the word that she used to describe herself. Forever pensive in her thoughts summed it all up. Now, mind you, she could use a variety of words, rather than the word, pensive. She could use the words, thoughtful, meditative, contemplative and brooding. She could use any of those synonyms instead of the word, pensive.

However, she did not.

Pensive was the word that she felt described her best. Pensive is a word with deep-rooted implications. It was in some way a word with a powerful tone, a rather somber word, a word to use only in carefully calculated sentences. On the other hand, one could also use it to describe a beautiful young woman sitting on her favorite park bench.

Alone.

She sat, watching birds peck around her feet. They were hoping that she had some morsels of food for them to enjoy. She did not have any food for the birds. The young woman did not come here to feed the birds.

It was never her intention to do so.

She did often wonder why she ignored the birds. Other bench dwellers here in the park did feed them and the birds knew that because they scattered about her feet, looking to feed off her. Perhaps she ignored them because she had nothing left to give them.

What little she had left she wanted to keep.

She often came here after her job working as an assistant to some pompous woman executive in the advertising agency in which she worked. It was all so exhausting and rather mindless; it bored her to tears, with deadlines, phone calls, preparation of endless reports, huffy, puffy customers with high opinions of themselves. In the big picture of life, it was all such mindless nonsense. Yet, she had to pay her bills and eat on occasion.

She came here to the park to feed her own soul. She came here to dream, to think, to wonder, and to recharge.

All she wanted to do was to sing. She wanted to be a superstar. An entertainer to sing on a stage somewhere.

It was her dream.

It was her passion from as far back as she could ever remember. She would put some tapes on in a little tape player she kept hidden in the basement of her home, and alone, when she thought no one was around and when she thought that no one was watching or listening, she would sing along with them, dance, whirl and twirl, all in quiet solitude of her own haven.

It was magic for her soul.

It was her dream.

When she did finally sing for her first audience, in one of

those silly elementary school functions, the audience went wild. Their reaction set her heart on fire! They stood up, cheered, clapped, and afterwards, they all told her how wonderful her voice was! It was captivating, soulful and strong.

All that was required now was for her parents to have an extra forty thousand dollars for tuition, and on top of that fee, to be able to fork over even more money, for her to live in apartment housing while she went to an elite, private and rather pretentious school.

That was all.

In order to learn how to sing, they told her, you would need to attend the school in order to learn how to sing.

She already could sing.

When you grow up rough and tumble in an inner city, your father is a tradesman, and your parents work and scrape for every dime they can find that was a dream that just was not going ever to have a chance of fulfillment. Now, she sat here, watching, waiting and wondering where it all had gone. All those dreams, all of those songs.

Lost forever.

Forever, lost in a haze, lost in a dream, a lost passion that will forever remain pensive within her heart.

Then there always was the man.

The man who captured her young heart, a man who she fell so deeply in love with, she could not stand it any longer.

And all too soon, he was gone too.

She sighed deeply; she exhaled and fought back against the tears. She closed her eyes and looked around, and he was there. He was always there, in every corner, in every aspect of her life. He haunted her and sometimes; she felt as if there was no escape. She stood up, moved to the other side of the park bench.

Yes! A different position on the same bench and he will be gone.

No, he is still there, right in front of her, smiling.

"Hey, I see you are having some trouble there with your skates!" Lilly McNeill turned around to see an older man smiling at her, as he looked down towards the trouble that she was having with one lace on her skate boot that just would not stay tied. She could not help but think, my goodness; he might be ten or so years older than I am, but what a good-looking man! He was tall, clean-cut, with a perfectly shaped jaw line and masculine facial features. He captivated her, and she stumbled over her words.

"Oh, yes. I mean, no! It is just this one lace. It will not stay tied."

He reached over, and then he knelt down on the ice. As he noticed that she was struggling to make a vain attempt to tie the troublesome lace.

"Here, please, let me help you."

He spoke softly to her, while he leaned over to assist her, "It is cold tonight, and pardon me for being so bold to suggest, but you might do better lacing your skates tighter, if you removed your mittens. I have noticed you stop and tie this same lace at least five times before."

She leaned back and steadied herself on the wall of the ice rink, and she watched as he pulled her skate boot gently into his hands. He removed his gloves and tied her troublesome lace. She studied him carefully while he laced her skates. She marveled at how handsome he was, as well as his profound and deep masculinity. His voice had a unique softness to it, yet a manly sound too, a sound in which she could not categorize. Being a singer at heart, she focused upon voices.

Then she realized as she gave it some more thought—how would he know that this was the fifth time this lace had given her trouble? She smiled and asked, while already being quite cognizant as to what the answer would be.

"Excuse me, but how would you know this is the fifth time, in which I have stopped to tie this particular skate lace?"

He pulled the lace tight, looped the top lace over the rest of them, and squeezed them gently into a double knot. He looked up and stared into her eyes.

He smiled, and my, oh my, what a wonderful smile he had! Standing up, he held her hand to steady her, while she gathered her skates underneath her and he said, "Because, I have been watching and admiring you the entire time. I am also quite good at counting, even from afar. Hi, I am, Jay Kelly. Actually, Master Sergeant Jay Kelly. I am in the United States Army Reserve. Well, part-time, that is. Full time, I am the co-owner of a music store with a good friend of mine."

He waved his arms around his head as if he wanted to include the surroundings within his next statement.

"Well, at least here in the civilian world that is!"

His smile welded inside of her heart and her mind's eye forever.

She had heard the term of a "whirlwind romance" used before; after all, she watched the movies and television too. However, she never experienced it before and she never dreamed what it could be like.

She was about to find out.

From the first day, the two of them met at that outdoor skating rink underneath a glowing Christmas tree—they never were apart for very long.

He was about ten years or thereabouts, older than she was, but in the big picture, their age difference mattered very little. It was the connection that mattered.

Age is just a measuring stick, a barometer of some sorts. The true age of a person lies within their heart, in their soul, and in their mind.

Jay was indeed in the military reserves and he had served for many years. He signed on to serve his country when he was eighteen and he never looked back. Now, as he approached his mid-forties, he was considering and planning retirement from his military service. He warned of some rumbles of overseas tours before his final commitment ended, and he knew his area of military expertise was something that would be required, if the swirling rumors came to fruition. Lilly soon realized there was another strong connection between them.

Jay loved music.

All types of music, and in his civilian life, he collaborated with a boyhood friend of his to operate a music shop and retail business. They also were partners on a small music distribution business, they managed some local musician's careers, and together, the two friends operated a small recording studio within the city. Their store sold musical instruments, records, tapes, sheet music, musical accessories as well as recordings of local artists who utilized the studio to try to find their big break in life and in the music scene too.

It was a successful operation, and often an eclectic hangout of sorts for musicians and artists to gather to share music, ideas, and general chit chat.

Early on in their relationship, Lilly and Jay shared a romantic dinner at Jay's apartment. After dinner, Lilly, while they shared some small talk and cordials, finally admitted to Jay that she loved to sing. She also confessed to Jay her dream, since she was a little girl, was to someday sing and to entertain professionally. She told him how it made her heart happy and singing filled her with joy.

Jay was thrilled!

"Really, Lilly? Why did you not tell me this before? You know what a big part of my life music is! Please sing for me, please?"

"No, Jay, I am embarrassed. I have not been singing so much these days. I took voice lessons for years, but my parent's money dried up, life ran over the top of me, I filled my heart with regrets over past mistakes and I gave it all up."

Jay stared at Lilly, and he studied her eyes. He could tell that singing was deep within her soul. It was part of her, and it was her passion.

"Please . . . I have something for you to sing."

Jay rushed over to a drawer in his kitchen and he opened it and pulled out some sheet music. He held it in his hand and waved it in the air while Lilly watched him.

He asked her, "Can you read music?"

"Yes, I can. I have quite a few years of education with a music school in addition to those voice lessons too."

"Good! Now, I am a very poor guitar player, but I can try to get through this piece. It is somewhat amazing, but a stranger came by and he dropped off this music in the store the other day. I never saw him before, an older guy, very well dressed. He did not say a word to anyone. He walked in and pinned it to the bulletin board where many of our local songwriters drop off music they have penned. He tipped his hat, smiled at me and walked out of the store without saying a word to anyone."

Jay handed some sheets to Lilly for her to study them as he motioned for them to head towards the living room. Lilly studied the music while she slowly followed behind Jay as he moved into the living room.

Jay picked up his six-string acoustic guitar, pulled a chair closer to an end table, sat down, and he started to check the tuning on his instrument.

"Here, Lilly. Please set the sheet music there on the end table, and you and I can share the sheets."

Lilly looked up and smiled, as she commented, "Jay, the words are beautiful to this song. The title alone gives me chills. 'Forever Pensive.' It is wonderful."

Jay nodded, ran his hands over the strings one more time to test the tuning, and he said, "Wait until you hear the melody. One of the piano players played it this afternoon in the store on the display piano, and it is haunting. It is a shame that the stranger did not leave his name and neglected to sign the music. It simply has a date of a week or so ago and is signed anonymously with traditional music credit. It is really a shame. I am not sure what traditional music this melody comes from, I know a great deal of music, as do my partner and people who frequent the store. No one ever heard this particular tune before."

Lilly now was intrigued, and she spread the music out on a table in front of them. Jay sat in the chair, held his guitar in his lap, and as Lilly moved in closer to look over his shoulder, he looked up.

"Ready?"

Lilly nodded to indicate that she was ready.

"Stick with me here. I am not a very good player. I will play it through once or twice and please, jump in on my signal once I have it rolling."

Jay started playing and after a few starts, stops, and missing a few notes, he made it through the melody without any errors.

In reality, he played a pretty mean guitar.

Lilly joined in upon his signal and there in that small apartment, they made wonderful music together. Lilly sang the tune magnificently; it seemed as if the stranger wrote the tune especially for her. It flowed from her so naturally, and she handled the structure of the song effortlessly, controlling her breathing and the delivery just right, as if she knew the tune beforehand and had sung it a million times before.

It was an astonishing moment, frozen in time, and it was stunning!

When they finished the song, they both looked at each other in a stunned silence, at first smiling, and then glowing, in the glory of how the song had resonated within their hearts. Jay placed his guitar down; he pulled Lilly in close to him and the two lovers passionately kissed. He then stood up and they held each other tightly.

He whispered to her, "Lilly, geez, my love. You are beyond fabulous. Not only, are you captivating and gorgeous, but you have the voice of an angel. You are a goddess. You must sing, always, always, always. Always sing, Lilly. Never stop."

They held onto each other tightly for a long time, until Jay asked her, "Now, can you sing some more for me?"

She smiled and nodded. She was secretly hoping he would ask her to continue to sing.

"Tell me what to play. I know some of my favorites. What are yours?" Lilly rattled off a number of popular tunes for Jay to play. Lilly sang along to the songs and their joy filled the apartment on this special night.

They laughed, they sang, and they held each other as the night whiled away. Until later that night in the apartment, they solidified their connection forever. Now, they were two lovers frozen in time together, sharing each other, sharing their hearts, their minds, their hopes and their dreams.

Their love was now deep, profound, and powerful.

Lilly's parents thought the relationship was pure foolishness. He was an older man, and in addition, he was in the military reserves, away on duty quite often. They felt, why waste your years on a man so much older, when with your beauty and personality, you could pick out any young man that you would want?

"You are young, beautiful, with men asking you for dates every day! Why waste your time on a soldier, a man who has lived so much more than you have? A man who already knows the ways of the world, in which you have never experienced? You need to meet a young man, fall in love and grow up together." They often preached to Lilly about how the relationship was doomed and presented many reasons as to why she should seek a man that is closer to her own age.

However, in this great, big world, we all know that love

knows no boundaries, there is no right, and there is no wrong.

There is only what you feel in your own heart.

Your own heart, when it all comes down to it, is the only place that counts.

The two lovers shared nights of unbridled passion. No lover was ever his equal, and she never felt as she did right now with him. She coveted how she felt while in his arms and in his protection.

Lilly was in love and this was her man. He made her whole; only with him was she able to shelve her usual pensive feelings. They were gone, evaporated, and nonexistent when Jay was around her. He even encouraged her to sing again, and he pushed her beyond her boundaries.

He was her biggest fan!

When Jay's partner heard her sing, "Forever Pensive," he insisted, along with Jay, that Lilly come into the studio and record the song. They did, and with only an acoustic six-string guitar, and some piano and Lilly singing, they laid the tracks down.

The results had all of them enthralled. It was now time to peddle the recording, and Jay made it his personal mission to do so.

Jay now knew that he was due for a military rotation overseas, into a combat zone in the never-ending madness known as the Middle East of this sad world; therefore, he knew time was of the essence. Before he had to leave for his duty, he worked relentlessly for Lilly, to convince music executives to listen to the recording, to arrange try-outs and auditions, mailing letters and stuffing envelopes with recorded tapes of the performance, a biography, and photos of Lilly.

He worked tirelessly, in an all-out effort for her finally to reach a person who would allow her to display her talents.

As so often happens in this mysterious world, timing is

often either spot on, or so poorly timed. One wonders why things happen as they do.

Who or what really controls how all of this happens?

Jay's military gear now lay packed and lying on the floor of his apartment. His orders tucked in one of those ominous brown envelopes, his date to ship out sealed, his commitment stamped and signed.

It was what he did.

He served to make this world a better place. It was his call to duty, a part of his honor, part of his soul, as much as singing was a part of his lover's soul.

The long-awaited call finally came on the morning of the day before he would ship out. It came from an executive of a recording company, in which Jay had, about three months earlier, sent the recording of "Forever Pensive" to, along with his usual promotional materials. The executive had been impressed. As a result, he arranged for a meeting, and then some preliminary auditions, in a studio on a date about one month after Jay would have already left for duty.

Out of the hundreds of calls, letters, meetings, why did this one come now?

Jay wanted to be there with Lilly to share in her joy; to share in what Jay knew would be her ultimate success. Everyone agreed upon the arrangements, the date haggled on a bit, but the executive did not waver, and you did not risk losing excellent opportunities such as this one was over a date. Jay knew his partner would go with Lilly and support her in his absence. When Lilly heard the news, it was, of course, a bittersweet moment of calculated joy. To have finally reached this moment in time and to have to face it without Jay was not exactly what Lilly wanted.

Still, after many hours of heart wrenching discussions, Lilly knew it was the moment she dreamt of and the opportunity was priceless. She would do it for her, for Jay, and for her essence. It would fulfill her passion and suppress her pensiveness forever more!

One last night of passion, more moments frozen in time, tearful goodbyes, tears that seemed as if they would not stop, memories and visions imbedded in their minds, uplifted and reinforced by promises to write, promises to send photographs, and then the ultimate promise, with a ring slipped on her finger, followed by a promise of a joyful return.

And therein is the tragedy because the return never came, at least not in the manner planned.

A knock at the door did come. A soldier in dress uniform accompanied by a color guard, a letter of sorrow, a box of medals, followed by a flag-draped coffin.

In times such as these, it seems, as if there are not enough tears in the entire world. Grief rains down upon you, as if Heaven exploded along with your heart and your inner being.

Lilly did not keep the appointment with the executive, and in fact, she never sang again.

The sun hid behind some dark clouds and Lilly looked up to see the previous sunny day, now covered with clouds. Slightly threatening clouds, darker in nature, yet moving quickly across the sky, which created a strange feeling of an ominous presence within her pensive heart. She wiped away some tears and noticed that with the arrival of the clouds, her visions of Jay were gone. He no longer stood in front of her smiling, and even some birds flew away.

They too must have realized that they could not take from her soul what did not exist.

Lilly stared off into the sky, lost in pensiveness.

At the entrance to the park, on the single pathway, strode a man. The man entered the gates of the park; he stopped and looked around as if he was reassuring himself as to his exact location. He adjusted the wide-brimmed black hat that he wore upon his head. Once again, he started to walk and then he adjusted his pace to stride along even quicker than he previously had.

He walked with a purpose.

And he walked with a mission.

His eyes locked straight forward, never wavering, never moving. Passersby stared at him, bench dwellers waved; dog walkers controlled their dogs who tried hard to greet him, and joggers in the park carefully jogged around him, all catching a glimpse of the man; while remaining captivated by his presence and his purpose. All of them, for some reason, tried to lure the man into a tip of the hat, a kind greeting or just an acknowledgement. Yet, it was all in vain.

For some unknown reason, the man did not move his eyes to acknowledge anyone or anything.

He was dressed all in black, with sharply creased black trousers, a black shirt, and all he wore as an overcoat of sorts, was a black leather vest, in which he left unbuttoned except for the last button just above his waist. On his head was a black hat with a wide brim, which he pulled down close to his ears, but you could still make out some of his facial features.

On his feet were black, sharp-tipped, highly polished boots, with metal clips on the edges that made a distinct clicking noise as he walked along the cold sidewalk. A neatly trimmed, black beard framed his handsome face and his facial features were striking, with a trimmed moustache that neatly lined his mouth. His clothes were made of the finest materials, not a single item was out of place, and not a hair on his head or his face was untrimmed or even slightly askew.

He walked with an air of confidence as he strode along. Everyone who noticed him could tell that this was a gentleman that was used to traveling around, and you could easily see that he was comfortable in many different surroundings.

He had dark, black, piercing eyes. Eyes that focused

straight ahead, his face was void of all expression; he had no emotions, and an aura of an ominous presence followed along behind him.

It seemed as if he had a mission, a mission of which nothing could derail.

He was the quiet stranger in the black hat.

He walked the pathway of the park for miles, up and down the winding corridors of asphalt and trees, along the rows of benches, never slowing, wavering or stopping, until he reached the bench in which Lilly sat upon, the bench where she pensively studied the world while it passed before her.

Just as she always did.

The quiet stranger in the black hat stopped in front of Lilly. He looked up at the sky, seemingly studying the arrival of the dark, black clouds, and then he looked at Lilly.

At first, Lilly did not notice him; she was lost in visions, lost in wayward journeys and dreams of Jay, music, and lost love, intermixed with tears. When she finally returned to this world, she noticed him, and at first the sight of him sent a cold shiver down her spine. Then she, for some reason, relaxed. She was not usually kind to strangers; she knew all too well the evil ways of this world and had the experiences and pain to prove it.

This stranger was somehow different and as she stood there studying him, her initial inclination to pick up and leave left her. She did not know why. Ordinarily, she would be long since gone by now. Her eyes went up and down his body; she studied his face, his immaculate clothes, the highly polished boots, his black hat, his handsome, captivating face and striking features.

Older man, yes, but he could astound a woman because he was so handsome! Then she met his eyes, piercing and dark, black, and set deeply in his head. They locked eyes, and she felt for some reason that she needed to smile at this quiet stranger in the black hat.

She did smile, and to a bit of her chagrin, he did not smile back. After what was in reality, only a few passing seconds, but seemed as if they were entire lifetimes. The stranger glanced at the end of the bench with his eyes. He leaned his hat over, and while looking at her over the top of his eyes, he pointed with his finger on his outstretched right hand, as if to ask permission to sit there.

The stranger still never spoke a single word.

Lilly followed his eyes and gesture, and without any apprehension, she spoke, "Please do."

She held her hand over the vacant place on the bench to emphasize the invitation. This was indeed unusual, because this was Lilly's bench and until now, she never shared it. Previously, whenever someone would come by and try to infiltrate her haven, she moved, because Lilly wanted nothing to do with interruptions to her pensive thoughts.

Now, for some reason, for which she could not understand or even begin to fathom, she knew that she needed to share her haven with this quiet stranger.

He nodded as if to thank her and gently sat down on the end of the bench. He sat there and said not a single word, but he too looked up at the sky again, as if he was still somewhat puzzled by how or why the dark clouds had moved in so quickly on the previously bright and sunny sky.

Lilly, at first, tried to ignore him, but she found herself studying him out of the corner of her eyes and she could not take her eyes off the stranger. He sat in silence, not moving much, even when a gentle wind worked against them while gracefully moving the rim of his black hat.

She suddenly felt the need to speak, as if the silence required a holiday, "Strange . . . how those dark clouds moved in so quickly on that blue sky."

Lilly pointed to the sky and then she looked over to the

quiet stranger for his reaction.

There was no reaction. He moved not a muscle and stared straight ahead.

Okay, she thought. This is weird. My voice and smile usually cracks the ice of every man I ever met. Now she moved a bit on the bench and felt this might be a challenge to conjure a reaction from this handsome stranger.

After all, she was a gorgeous young woman, and he *did* sit next to her!

Lilly changed the tone of her voice to a softer and somewhat slightly provocative inflection. She was and will always be a singer.

"I have never seen you in the park before. Do you walk here often?"

Nothing but the same stare, the same silence.

Okay now, a shift of her legs, a little lean towards him, a flicker of her eyes . . . damn, this is a good-looking man.

"I love this park. I come here often. In fact, if the weather is nice, I come here every day after work. It helps me clear my mind from my job."

Nothing but the same stare, same silence, same lack of reaction. Yet, for some reason, Lilly still tried to provoke conversation or some type of reaction from the quiet stranger in the black hat. She suddenly felt the overpowering need to share a deeper thought.

To a stranger!

A stranger, in which she ordinarily would never even speak to or even interact with, nonetheless, shared her sacred park bench with on this now very strange afternoon.

Even a man as attractive as he was.

"My job scatters my thoughts. It does not make me happy. Solitude and pensive reflection here in this park. Now that does not make me happy either, but it does for some reason, calm my soul quite a bit. I keep searching, searching for happiness. I had a man who made me happy, happier than I ever dreamed possible, but he is gone now and really. . .."

Lilly's voice drifted off. Raw and pure emotion captured it. The tears came back, even darker clouds moved back in on the sky above them. She bowed her head to hide her eyes and reaction from the quiet stranger in the black hat.

She felt it was time to leave; this quiet stranger was not going to speak, nor would he even react.

She feigned looking at a nonexistent watch, picked up her purse and said, "Well, I did not realize the time. Goodbye and have a nice day."

She reached for her purse and went to stand up, when to her utter shock and surprise, the quiet stranger spoke. A deep, melodious voice came out of him. It was a voice, in which to a singer such as Lilly was, immediately became captivating to her.

He said, "You are wrong, Lilly. He never left you."

A cold shiver resonated through Lilly as she settled back down and looked over at the stranger. Their eyes locked upon each other. Piercing, dark eyes that were seeing right into her inner soul. Lilly thought, 'How does he know her name? Who the hell is this man?'

Lilly sat there shivering in unbridled oneness with this quiet stranger as he continued to peel the layers of pain away, "He is always with you. Love as you shared and still share, never dies, it transcends time, space and all obstacles. You need to be happy. He wants nothing more than for you to be full of joy forever. What you do not recognize, is that you locked your own destiny long, long ago. You need to sing. Until you do, you will remain forever pensive. It is your gift to this world. It is your gift to him, for you to sing, for you to be happy. He will be laughing as you sing, in the highest plane, a place, in which your greatest dreams cannot fathom. When you sing, you will sing not only for the world but also for you and for him. Soul mates never leave one another, not now, not even at the end of all time."

The quiet stranger in the black hat finished speaking. He leaned back on the support of the park bench; he reached inside of his vest and pulled out some papers.

Lilly was speechless, the tears poured from her eyes, she could not stop staring at the quiet stranger. She followed his movements while he slowly stood up and handed her the papers from his vest.

He looked up at the sky, and pointed, while saying, "You see, the sky is now blue again, the dark clouds are leaving, and the sun is shining, because for lovers such as you and Jay are, your hearts always remain open. Always remain connected forever. There is no escape, Lilly. None. Now sing, now smile, and continue to make your heart happy and Heaven will rejoice along with you."

He smiled, tipped his hat, turned, and then walked briskly away.

Lilly still did not move. Instead, she sat in silence, in tears of mixed joy and pain leaving her spirit.

Lilly then suddenly smiled, and she watched until he left her view and she could no longer hear the click of the metal tips of his boots on the walkway.

She opened the papers in which he had given her and even before she glanced at them, she knew what they would be. She smiled and wiped the tears away that fell from her eyes onto the sheet music.

The tears landed upon the title of the song, "Forever Pensive."

Jay was back, standing in front of her in the now bright sunlight, smiling his special smile to her.

She heard him say, "How much he loved her."

Then she recalled Jay telling her, "It is somewhat amazing, but a stranger came by and he dropped off this music in the store the other day. I never saw him before, an older guy, very well dressed. He did not say a word to anyone, he walked in and pinned it to the bulletin board where many of our local songwriters drop off music they have penned. He tipped his hat, smiled at me and walked out of the store without saying a word to anyone."

She folded the sheet music and held them close to her heart while whispering aloud, "Well Jay, he finally spoke to both of us."

Three years later, Lilly McNeil, the superstar entertainer, tried very hard to leave somewhat clandestinely from a side entrance of the venue in which she just played to another sold-out audience.

The flashbulbs popped, reporters stuck microphones in her face, and fans screamed her name and waved papers in her face, in an attempt to lure her into signing an autograph or two. Her bodyguards protected her and shielded her, but remarkably out of all the bedlam, Lilly heard the solitary shouts of a young girl from the crowd. A young girl who pleaded with her in a captivating and soulful voice. When she heard the voice of the young fan, Lilly suddenly was back in her basement singing to cassette tapes while all alone in her dreams.

Singing, all alone.

On the other hand, was she?

"Please! Please, Lilly. I am a singer too! I sing to myself, alone, in my room, I want to be just like you!"

Lilly stopped, and her bodyguards tried hard to convince her to keep moving. She ignored them; she took the paper from the young girl and smiled at her.

She signed it, handed it back to the young girl and said, "When you sing and smile, you are never alone. Never stop singing and smiling, because when you sing and smile, you make your own heart happy and Heaven will rejoice along with you."

The bodyguards whisked her away, and they moved Lilly quickly towards the rear door of the limousine waiting at the curbside. Lilly was just about to duck down and slide into the rear seat when she spotted him.

He was there, in the shadows, outside of the flash of the

bright lights, he was watching and waiting.

Just on the other side of the rope fence, *he* was there. She somehow always knew that someday he would return.

There he was, the quiet stranger in the black hat.

He smiled at her, and their eyes locked.

"Wait! No. Stop!" Lilly screamed as she muscled away from her entourage and walked slowly over to the rope to speak with him. She waved for her guards to stay their distance. This was a private moment.

When she reached him, she held out her hands over the top of the rope and the quiet stranger took them gently in his.

"I have no idea who, or perhaps, even what, you are. To be honest, I would rather not know. I think that you might be an angel, my guardian angel perhaps, or maybe a spirit or a soul whom I contracted with a long time ago, but regardless, thank you."

The stranger did not say a word; instead, he smiled and held her hands tighter.

Lilly felt the warmth of his hands and as she looked into those magical eyes, she asked, "Did you write the song? I have to know where the song came from."

The quiet stranger in the black hat finally went to speak and before he spoke, as a prelude to his words, he gently shook his head to indicate that he did not write the song.

He said, "No. I have a few talents here in this world that I presently reside in but, no, I could never write such a beautiful song. No one person of this world, or any other world, could ever write such a remarkable song. You wrote it with Jay. Your love wrote it together. It is a song from your own hearts. A melody of love, entwined forever more with the two of you. You see, my dear Lilly, in this entire world, love, happiness, and your own heart, are the only things that really count. Time and space and angst and pensiveness, it all means nothing, whenever it is compared to those three, special things."

The quiet stranger in the black hat loosened his grip on Lilly's hands; he smiled, tipped his hat and turned to walk briskly away.

Lilly stood there watching, with a tear in her eye and the song upon her heart. She stood and watched for a long time until he disappeared into the night and she could no longer hear the click of the metal tips of his boots upon the pavement.

THE END

The Gypsy

"Ohhhhhhh . . . Miss Wainwright! I foresee a great event coming for you in the very near future! A new horizon, a new man perhaps . . . or something else. The glass is foggy yet, and the visions are not yet clear. It is a vision in the making, a new adventure or a new person. No, no, let's look deeply into the mysterious glass! I think that it might be a new business venture!"

The gypsy, or as she was known on the main drag in this small city by her glowing neon sign in the small storefront window, "The Great and All-Knowing, Ms. Lolita," waved her hands over a crystal ball glowing in front of her on a table.

While Ms. Lolita waved her hands and focused into the magical glass, she occasionally rolled her eyes back into her head and leaned back into her chair. Ms. Lolita, then, in a seemingly deep trance-like state, leaned back in, in order to stare once again deeply in the crystal.

The crystal that held all the secrets within its glowing mystery!

What the unsuspecting customer, the humble, extremely wealthy and slightly naïve, Miss Wainwright did not notice, was that while Ms. Lolita leaned back, rolled her eyes and then refocused on the glowing crystal, Ms. Lolita occasionally picked her eyes up and she was actually studying Miss Wainwright's every move and her every motion.

The "gypsy" fortune teller was carefully studying body,

eyes and facial language for a "hit" or a twitch, or some type of signal from Miss Wainwright, based upon what the all-knowing Ms. Lolita had just spoken to her.

'Geez, shit, no hit yet. All this stupid battleaxe does is to stare endlessly into the glass. Okay . . . here, let's try this one.' Ms. Lolita thought to herself, while she leaned back for another round of "magically enhanced," observations after searching Miss Wainwright for clues.

The mysterious and powerful Ms. Lolita leaned in and with her left foot carefully concealed underneath the red tablecloth, she carefully pressed down with her foot on a pedal located on the floor. While she waved her hands wildly over the crystal ball, she pushed the lever and the mechanism attached to the pedal, made the table slowly rise into the air. Slowly, gradually, it rose in the air, all while Ms. Lolita was vigilantly watching Miss Wainwright for some type of clue.

Ms. Lolita feigned her deepest, trance-like state, and she spewed ominously in her patented indecipherable babble of her supposed trance.

"Oh! Wow! Bam! Zoom! Blackberry wine!"

"Oh, my, Ms. Lolita! The table is rising." the naïve spinster, Miss Wainwright somewhat, shakily observed.

In strict accordance with Ms. Lolita's instructions, despite the intense pressure of the power of the magic, Miss Wainwright managed to keep her folded hands firmly upon the now levitating table.

After all, we would not want to risk a shattering of the magical spell.

Ms. Lolita continued with her deepest trance, she reached over and threw some magic sawdust into the air. She turned the hidden knob under the table to float more burning incense into the air, all while still babbling on and on in her best incantations.

Slowly, Ms. Lolita relieved the pressure on the table lever. The table descended back down to the floor and she leaned back intensely, still studying the crystal ball.

"Let's give this another shot now," the phony gypsy thought to herself.

She spoke once again in English, after a dramatic roll of her eyes, in order to recover from her trance, "I see a man now. He is clearer within my visions . . . dark hair, maybe . . . a little bald in the front."

Here we go now . . . pay dirt!

"Oh yes, that is the man you mentioned last week when you read my palm. I think it might be the man who services my automobile, he was very nice, and he seemed quite interested in me too," Miss Wainwright had shown a chink in her armor and now that was all, Ms. Lolita required to move in for the kill shot.

"Yes, it is! The man whom I foresaw in your palm last week. The man at the automobile service center. He smiles easily. He is handsome, single, and he is interested in you. I see him studying you as you walk away. He is admiring your fabulous figure. I think it might be a love for you that I foresaw."

"Oh my, how embarrassing. I did not realize he was watching me so intensely. He *is* a handsome man!"

"What is it that will happen to us, Ms. Lolita?"

Ah, sorry. Not quite so fast, Miss Wainwright. Unfortunately, it does not work that way. Magical transmissions from far-off lands and spheres outside our normal realms do not come so easily, nor do they come so cheaply either.

"Ooh, no! The visions are growing darker and darker! You must have some inner mind blockage, Miss Wainwright. It is some hidden, dark secret deep within your spirit, which is preventing me from seeing the entire picture, and the ball is . . . fading."

As Ms. Lolita spoke the words, she slowly rotated the hidden knob under the table to shut down the light underneath the glowing magical predictor of all fate, as well as shutting down the intensity of the incense control.

Incense is not free either.

"Oh my," Miss Wainwright fretted at the sight of the disappearing glow of the powerful crystal, "I thought I had cleared my mind of all those thoughts. It must be so deep inside of me that even I cannot detect it."

With that, Ms. Lolita stood up. She walked over to the light switch and snapped on the overhead lights in the small store. The lights flickered to life and the remaining smoke of the burning incense danced and floated in a magical haze within the room.

"I am sorry, Miss Wainwright, but we do grow closer and closer to the truth. I think for our next session we will combine the power of the crystal ball with the palm readings and even try some hypnosis. Perhaps then, we can clear these deep and profound blockages from within your mind."

"Oh, I agree. Whatever you suggest, Ms. Lolita, will that session cost some more money for my fee?"

Ms. Lolita whipped up her best regrettable frown and changed her voice to convey an air of phony sympathy, "I am afraid to say that it will. I will need to bring in an assistant to help me with the hypnosis. We will need to combine my powers with the Great Randolfski. He is, after all, world-renowned. I will need to check his availability and call you with the payment amounts as soon as I hear back from him. That way, you can bring along a check and we can pay him for his services. My meager services and abilities, well, they pale in comparison to the Great Randolfski."

"Oh well, I understand. Oh, my, I will need to retain the services of such an expert! Yes, I agree—whatever it takes, here, here, here, is a check for today with a tad extra for your insight. I will be back next week, or should I come sooner and more often?"

"Well, Miss Wainwright, I think we should go with

every other day, at least until all of us together manage to clear these obstacles. I regret that we must cut this short now. I do have other appointments."

Ms. Lolita took the check from Miss Wainwright, slipped it down inside her brassiere. She then gently grabbed Miss Wainwright by her hand and guided her out the front door. All the time, Ms. Lolita was consoling her as to how to cope with her pressure and stress, until they could meet again and finally, for the last time, they could discover together the secrets of her somewhat shrouded future.

When the door closed behind Miss Wainwright and the confused spinster had pulled away in her expensive luxury automobile, Ms. Lolita reached over, turned the key in the door and turned out the blinking neon sign in the front window. She rested her head upon the door and sighed deeply. Bilking lonely spinsters out of their life savings was a bit exhausting.

A curtain along the side of the reading room parted, and a tall, lanky man appeared. He smiled from ear-to-ear and he held in his one hand a bottle of whiskey, and in his other hand, he held two glasses. A lit cigarette dangled precariously from his lips.

"Here, all-knowing one, you look as if you need a drink. I need to prepare. After all, the Great Randolfski needs to be on top of his game too! I have a grand entrance to make next time. I loved that part where you told her the man at the service center was checking her out as she walked away. A woman, who looks like a half-eaten pear, wears blue wigs and has eyeglasses as thick as soda bottles. Ha! I do not think so! Now, you on the other hand, let me reach down inside that marvelous chest of yours and claim not only that check, but some other things too." He lifted his eyes seductively towards Ms. Lolita as a prelude to some slightly, uninhibited intentions that he harbored.

The man set the bottle and the two glasses upon the table and pulled a chair over to sit down. He took the cap off the bottle and poured two drinks in the glasses. Ms. Lolita shook her head and slowly walked to the table to join the man.

She spoke softly, almost as if she was afraid of someone else listening in, "Yes, well, it was not easy this go around. I think I overdid the incense, but I could not get her to crack. I think I am losing my touch after all of these years of dealing with these kooks who wander in here."

Ms. Lolita pulled the chair out, sat down, and she took the glass in her hands. She tilted the glass back and took a long swig. She pulled her blouse down, as well as her brassiere, exposed her breasts to the man, removed the check, and handed it to the man with a coy smile.

"Here is the check. As far as the rest of the probing down there—it will have to wait until later. I am exhausted. Steve, can you please look at that lever for the table? I told you last week that it was hard to push down. I was turning blue in the face, trying to hold that stupid table up."

"I see that you are full of love. I will look at it first thing tomorrow, Ann. I promise. You know Ann, no pressure here. However, we have to get this dough from this old bird. We need the thousand bucks by next week, or you know it is not gonna be pretty."

Ms. Lolita, or now, specifically, or more factually, Ann Lolita, nodded her head, waved her hand and spoke softly while motioning to Steve to refill her glass.

"I know, I know, I know, I will get it. I wish you would stop playing those ponies. You get us in trouble all the time and soon, they will all be calling for the money you owe them. Don't worry, together, we will soon have her forking over her house, her car notes, everything. I promise. Just like that other weirdo. What was his name? I let him stare down my blouse all the time, and he handed the money over right and left. Too bad, he keeled over before we hit the big payoff!"

She smiled, threw down the next shot, and she then waved to Steve.

"Now, come to think of it, I feel refreshed! How about a bit of that probing, big guy?"

That night, after a bit of a whiskey-induced frolic or two with Steve and some smokes from a lot more than just the incense that floated around the store, Ann sat wide-awake in a chair in their bedroom.

Steve snored loudly; sound asleep in the bed in front of her in the darkness. She often wished she picked a better boyfriend than this particular one on this go around, but he was loyal, and a great con man too. He was not that bad looking, a worthy partner for a roll or two in the hay, and he did make her laugh on rare occasions. She could do without his habit of betting on the horses and numbers too much and wasting their money, but overall, he was not too bad.

She had worse. . ..

Ann sat in the darkness, dragging deeply on a cigarette, thinking where this all went so wrong, where her life went so far astray that she could not even remember what her goals were or where she originally started out.

Ann Lolita was gorgeous, a beauty queen, the star of the show. She was captain of her cheerleading squad in high school; she could have her pick, anytime, anywhere, of any of the young men. Ann had an attractive figure, with a slim waist that gradually flowed into gentle curves and hips that rocked young men's worlds. She had wonderful features, olive skin, unblemished by a mark or flaw, gorgeous black hair tumbling down over her shoulders.

Queen of the prom, queen of hearts.

Somehow, it all went away, lost in a maze of time.

Besides her physical beauty, she also had other talents. She was highly creative, an artist, above all, she always was an artist. Even as a little girl, she could pick up a pencil and draw people, animals, landscapes, anything. No formal training, no effort, all miraculous, God-given talent. She could draw anywhere, any time.

Remarkable talent. . ..

She was indeed a phony gypsy! She actually grew up outside of Hartford in Connecticut, a family of Italian Americans, her mom was a schoolteacher, and her dad worked as a mid-level executive in a Connecticut utility company. She grew up happy, with a nice house, no brothers or sisters. She was an only child, but she was happy. All of her teachers in school encouraged her to go on to pursue the arts in a university, and she did. She went off to Philadelphia, to a university there, which had studies focused upon the arts as well as general studies. Ann took theatre, art, and drama classes. Her drawings won awards, glowing reviews and seemingly endless praise of her remarkable skills. Her professors posted them in the university's galleries and she was on her way.

Then, in her junior year at the university, in an off-campus drama production of which she had a supporting role in, she met him. He was there watching, observing, keeping an eye on local talent. An agent, a man of the world, a man with connections. Ann had caught his eye, and after the play, he spoke to her, filled her head with glory and entranced her with dreams of Broadway, Hollywood, television, the big lights, the red-carpeted runways! He was older, but extremely good-looking, smooth talking, and to be honest, rather ill intentioned.

He captivated her. After ample wine, romance and dining in fancy restaurants, rides in fancy cars, a few nights of bedroom antics and passion, he lured her away, and she left school to a howl of protest from her professors, her friends and her parents. She left behind the drawings, the art, the hope and the dreams.

Sadly, Ann Lolita left the largest part of her soul hanging on walls in those galleries.

Now, her new agent did have connections, and he did

manage to obtain a few minor acting roles for Ann. They crisscrossed the nation, first in New York City, then Atlanta, then to Chicago, and finally, just when the money ran out, they ended up in California.

Along the way, he also picked up a bad drug habit and Ann, in frustration, left him and went out on her own to pursue the dream.

A dream which never came.

A few more minor roles, a number of attempts of working her way to the top by seducing various executives in key positions, all failures and all too soon; the dream was dead.

Lost in a dusty memory, along with her drawings.

Ann finished her cigarette; she snuffed it out in the ashtray and watched as the smoke from the dying flame spiraled around the tray. Even in the dim light of the bedroom, she could see it there, whispering gently into the air. Sadly, signaling to her, of how her dreams were dying embers now, too.

She leaned back, sighed and thought how strange this life is. How did a chance encounter of sorts at a carnival turn into a career as a con artist? She reached for the pack of cigarettes and the cigarette lighter, and she lit one more.

'One more smoke and I will go to sleep,' she thought.

As she lit the cigarette, she could clearly see herself entering the tent of the gypsy fortune teller set up in the corner of the carnival. There, in some type of quiet desperation, she was seeking to know her future, her destiny. Her dreams were now dead. But could this strange woman from another time or another place, or another spiritual plane, be able to advise her of which direction to go?

After dropping a few dollars in the jar, the old gypsy rattled some beads, chanted some magical incantations, "Ohhwowe, bammlota, zooombaki, kilita, HUCKENY!"

She waved incense in the air and threw sawdust into the

sunlight to see what patterns it would create when it landed on the table.

Patterns to foretell what lies ahead for Ann.

That is how far we fall sometimes in this life, to where we no longer follow our hearts and we are willing to allow sawdust falling from the sky to guide our instincts and directions.

Now, Ann was an artist and an actress, and while she had fallen from the grace of her previous glory, she still was very good at what she did.

The old gypsy did have some points that she was correct about in Ann's past, but nothing of any significance, and as far as her future predictions, Ann did not buy any of it.

No one *in this world* can tell of a complete stranger's past or foretell what lies ahead for them.

She could tell a fellow actress when she met one.

She came away from the tent at the carnival, far from enlightened as to what her future held. Or perhaps, she did come away with her future.

She entered the tent as Ann Lolita and left as, "The Great and All-Knowing, Ms. Lolita."

Sadly, she never drew a sketch or picture again. Her bitterness would not allow her creative spirit loose.

Now, she lived a life that in her heart, she knew, was nothing more than a slow and quiet torture. She sat there in the quiet darkness and she snuffed out the cigarette in the ashtray. Ann watched as the glowing embers of the dying cigarette faded in the darkness, along with her own spirit that largely had faded too.

The next morning was the same as all the others. Or was it?

Ann turned the key in the front door of the storefront; she flipped the switch on for the neon sign in the window and watched as it flickered to life. It was the middle of April and the weather seemed to be decent enough, sunny and cold right now, but it was sure to warm up by the afternoon. Ann looked out the smoky front window of the store and wiped away some residue of the smoke from the incense that covered the glass.

"I really do need to clean this glass someday," Ann spoke aloud as she walked away. She lit some candles, turned the incense burners on, and sat down at the table.

Steve was behind the curtain, but she knew he would not work on the lever today. Right now, even without seeing Steve, Ann knew that he had the newspaper open and he was circling the selections for the horse races later on in the day.

After all, that was her "gift" to be able to predict the future.

Right after noontime, he would slip away, walk down to the bar on the corner and with the local bookie, place more bets for horses that will not win. In addition, all too soon, they would be calling for the money he owed them, in fact, in a day or two. . ..

The day passed along slowly, a few young college students stopped by for a palm reading or two for fun, a curious businessman searching for false hope stopped in for a reading. He was obviously having an extramarital affair, and he was wondering if his mistress would eventually marry him, when his kids were finally grown and he could safely leave his wife.

All the usual drivel.

Miss Wainwright would be in for her big moment tomorrow afternoon; therefore, Ann did not expect too much from this particular day. It was all business as usual.

On the other hand; she thought it was.

Out on the streets, in the bright sunlight of a glorious April morning, the distinct click of metal tips of highly polished boots on a hard surface, mixed and echoed with the traffic rolling along the main street. The boots clicked loudly, because the man who wore them walked along the sidewalk at a rapid pace. He moved quickly and effortlessly through the crowds of browsing window shoppers; he maneuvered between dog-walkers, mothers pushing babies in strollers and shoppers carrying their newly purchased goods.

He walked by the outdoor fruit and vegetable market and ignored the shouts of the shopkeeper, peddling the fact that early season strawberries were on special this glorious April morning.

The man did not move his eyes to acknowledge anyone or anything. He was dressed all in black, with sharply creased black trousers, a black shirt, and all he wore, as an overcoat of sorts, was a black leather vest, in which he left unbuttoned except for the last button just above his waist.

On his head was a black hat with a wide brim, which he pulled down close to his ears, but you could still make out some of his facial features.

A neatly trimmed, black beard framed his handsome face and his facial features were striking, with a neatly trimmed moustache that lined his mouth. His clothes were made of the finest materials. Not a single item was out of place, not a hair on his head or his face, untrimmed or even slightly askew.

He walked with an air of confidence as he strode along. Everyone who noticed him could tell that this was a gentleman that was used to traveling around, and you could easily see that he was comfortable in many different surroundings.

He had dark, black, piercing eyes. Eyes that focused straight ahead, his face was void of all expression; he had no emotions, and an aura of an ominous presence followed along behind him.

It seemed as if he had a mission, a mission of which nothing could derail.

He was the quiet stranger in the black hat.

The quiet stranger strode along until he reached what appeared to be his destination. He stopped in front of the small, dingy storefront of, "The Great and All-Knowing, Ms. Lolita."

He stopped, and he spun around a few times as if he needed to adjust or somehow confirm his final direction and destination. His dark eyes spotted the sign in the window and for a few seconds, he stared at the sad, blinking, neon sign proclaiming her so-called talents to the entire world.

He adjusted his hat, pulling it down a bit more in the front of his face, in order to shield his eyes just a bit. He lowered his head, moved quickly and with a turn of the knob of the front door, he stepped into her lair.

When she heard the door open, Ms. Lolita looked up from her table and within seconds, she identified the potential of this particular customer. It was what she did because within seconds, she could analyze a potential bilking opportunity. Ms. Lolita seldom, if ever, missed her targets; yet, this time . . . she might just meet her match.

'Okay,' she thought, 'handsome, extraordinarily so and his eyes are so dark, and he has a tall, lean, powerful frame. My, he astounds you! He is well dressed in the finest clothes, a hat that must be worth a fortune alone, and look at those boots. Wow! This boring day has suddenly taken a surprising turn. This handsome man has some extra money to burn. My, he is so immense in stature. . ..'

She watched as he stood there for a second or two while she studied him. He looked around in the dark store, scanned the surroundings and then he settled his eyes upon her seated at the table.

She felt a cold shiver. His eyes and stare seemed to go right through to her soul. An aura of an ominous presence seemed to have come along with this handsome stranger.

Time to crank it up, Ann!

Do not allow this sucker to get away.

"Welcome stranger! Welcome to the reading room, a room that unlocks the secrets of your future, as well as the mysteries of your past. Come in, come in, sit, and let Ms. Lolita allow you to be in touch with your own inner spiritual awareness of your past, and let me reveal to you, your future fate!"

The stranger stood and stared at Ms. Lolita; however, he did not say a single word.

Ann thought to herself, 'Wow, . . . good-looking guy, but he might be a weirdo. I hope Steve has not left yet to place his pony bets. Although, this immense man would crush poor Steve with one sweep of his arm.'

After what seemed as if it were a lifetime, the stranger finally walked over to the table, he reached inside of his vest, took out a crisp, fifty-dollar bill and without saying a single word, he placed it into the jar on the table. He pulled out the chair, sat down opposite Ms. Lolita, and stared directly into her eyes.

Dark, piercing, black eyes, a large, yet lean frame. This was a big, powerful man and his ominous stare extremely unnerved Ann. He continued to send cold shivers up and down her entire body, and if he had not dropped that fifty-dollar bill in her jar, she decided that she would have asked him to leave.

There was something very strange and unnerving about this customer. And even with all of her experience, she could not place what it was with this man or what was so different about him.

Still, fifty bucks just bought a bit of her time, so she cranked it up, "What is it that brings you in today, dark stranger dressed in black, shall I read your palm, or look into the crystal ball, or perhaps, something deeper or darker?"

The quiet stranger in the black hat still did not speak, but with his right arm, he slowly reached out across the table and held his right hand out over the table, over the top of the crystal ball. While never unlocking his eyes or stare from Ms. Lolita, he slowly and gracefully turned his palm upside down in front of Ms. Lolita.

"Oh yes, read your palm, unlock the mysteries of life for you, quiet, dark stranger!"

She leaned back in her chair and rolled her eyes back as she started her usual, tedious act, and when she reached under the table to turn the knob for the on switch for the incense, she pulled back in shock, because the quiet stranger had met her hand under the table.

He already had his hand on the knob! He moved so fast! How did he put his hand under the table? How did he reach so far! It seemed as if he never moved a muscle!

Ms. Lolita's face erupted in shock, and she pulled her hands back and noticed the quiet stranger still held his other hand out in front of her. He still did not speak, but his eyes went from her eyes to his palm, and then back again. He was indicating to Ann for her to look at his palm.

She breathed deeply. She sighed, while she slowly and apprehensively, reached out to take his hand. When she did, she felt an incredible warmth emitting from his palm; it filled her with a glow, a strange sensation of pain and sorrow leaving her body. Ann shook it off quickly, flipped the reading glasses hanging on a chain around her neck up to her eyes, and she stared in. As she did, she saw the quiet stranger move his legs, and she felt the table rise! He must have his foot on her lever!

How could he even reach it? How did he know it was there?

She went to pull her hand away and end this charade, but the stranger held her hand tightly and finally spoke, in a low, yet melodious voice, "No, look at my palm, Ann. Just as the old gypsy did with you in that tent years ago, in the carnival. Read it!"

How did he know that? She trembled in fear now, but his grip was strong. She felt for a moment, as if she should cry out and pull hard to escape his grip, but her fear, for some reason, slowly subsided and she forced herself to look down at his hand. When she did, she gasped in shock, because to her horror, she saw it had no lines, it had no marks, and it was smooth and unblemished.

She dropped his hand in continued awe and shock, but he quickly took her hand back and gently grasped it, as if to assist in steadying her and to calm her. She felt faint. The room was spinning, and she felt her chest heaving, while she took deep breaths to prevent from fainting.

While she leaned in, she finally managed to whisper, "Just who the hell are you? What do you want?"

He gently let go of her hand, let the table back down, folded his hands in front of him and placed them on the table.

He spoke again, in his low, deep melodious voice, "Ann Lolita, born in Hartford, Connecticut, April twentieth, in the year 1955 at three ten in the afternoon. You have a loving family, your father was successful in his career, your mother is a loving woman, who taught children, and she loves you with all of her heart. Your mother cherishes the pencil drawing of your first puppy that you drew when you were seven years old. Your mother still has it in her drawer, in the top, left-hand corner of the roll-top desk in her living room. The drawer with the silver handle with the red inlay. You recall, which one I mean. Where she also keeps for safekeeping, the good luck charm of her own dear mother. Life ran over you, evil men swayed you and you gave up your passion in disillusion, in heartbreak, in a tent in some shady carnival."

He took a little breath, pierced her with his eyes, pointed with his finger and said, "You need to return to your passion, give up this sham of a life, and return to Miss Wainwright, all the money you have bilked her out of and share with the world, your gifts. You have too much love, beauty and talent to give to this tired, old world. Only when you share them, will you be set free."

Ann did not know what to say. She sat there in horror

and at first, she thought to call out to Steve for help, but she realized that he was already gone to place his bets, or he would have already rushed in to try to save her.

Save her from . . . what?

To save her from the truth?

To save her from her own past, or from her own dreams and desires?

Truth that remarkably somehow, or someway, this quiet stranger in the black hat has the insight to know and the courage to tell her.

How does he know? No one *in this world* can see the future or know the past!

He stopped speaking, smiled, and slowly outstretched his arm again over the table. He motioned with his eyes for her to take his hand. It seemed as if his mission now was to comfort her. Ann now had tears rolling down her cheeks, but she reached out and took his hand.

Instead, he flipped her hand over and studied *her palm.* "Number one, two, seven, Glenbrook Road. There is an art gallery and cultural arts center there. It is operated by a man whose last name is Jenkins. He is looking for an artist to sign to a contract. Mr. Jenkins is getting on in years and he is looking for a partner to work for him, he loves art, particularly, black and white pencil drawings. He longs to display quality pencil sketches of. . .."

He let go of her hand, reached inside of his vest, took out a piece of paper and a number of pencils. He placed them on the table, and then he slid them over to Ann.

He looked back up into her eyes and said rather forcibly, "Draw me."

She stumbled over her emotions; she wiped her eyes and tried hard to speak.

Finally, Ann managed to speak, and some fractured words came out, "I cannot. I have not drawn anything or anyone in years. I cannot do it. It is an old life, a lost dream and a missed opportunity."

"You are incorrect, Ann. The only missed opportunities in this life would be the ones we are too afraid of in order to recognize them. The first steps for a baby to take, are the hardest ones. The first words typed for writers, are the most difficult. The first notes sung for a singer are the most strained, the first awkward glances, the first kiss, and first fumbling embraces for lovers, are nearly impossible. They are all the hardest and after we conquer those, then it all becomes easier. It becomes magical."

Ann nodded. She studied his face, took the pencil, took the paper, and with her hands shaking and trembling, she steadied herself and started to sketch him. He did not move. He allowed her to study him, to capture his features, his amazing eyes, and his every detail.

It *was* magical.

While she drew, she felt the release of the pain. Her soul returned inside of her, her creativity restored, the exhilaration of an artist suppressed, the joy of her heart, her spirit and mind lost, then regained.

She was drawing again!

She sketched, and she sketched, and within what seemed as if it were only a few moments, she had captured the image of the quiet stranger in the black hat forever on a sheet of paper.

She finished, dropped the pencil, and picked up the piece of paper. After studying it, she smiled.

It was magnificent.

An outpouring of years of suppressed creativity had created a masterpiece. She also realized that the subject material was not exactly ordinary.

She held it up for the quiet stranger to see. He studied it for a long time, and without speaking, the stranger's eyes and smile displayed satisfaction with her creation. Before Ann could even react or speak, he then suddenly and without another word, stood up. He tipped his hat, turned and walked quickly out the front door of the store, while gently closing the door behind him.

Ann reached into the jar, took out the fifty-dollar bill, and held it tightly in her hand. She jumped out of her chair, rushed to the door, and flung it open.

She rushed out to the sidewalk; she called out onto the busy street and yelled to him, "Wait! Wait! I need to know your name. Here, please come back and take your money back!"

Ann could see him walking in the distance on the sidewalk, but he did not turn around or acknowledge her cries. She watched until he left her view, lost in the maze of humanity and business upon the city street. She stood there until she could no longer see him or hear the click of the metal tips of his boots on the sidewalk.

Glancing down at the fifty-dollar bill in her hand, she realized that where he came from, and to where he was going, he most likely did not need it.

Ten months later, on a late Saturday afternoon, the Glenside Gallery and Cultural Arts Center was the center of activity.

A cold February day was not ideal for outdoor activities, but in the glow and warmth of-the-art gallery, it was a perfect day for viewing fine art and inspirational collections. That is exactly what the communities of artists, art collectors, and art lovers were doing on this day. A jam-packed gallery, filled with people sipping wine and sampling cheese, while viewing the artwork, all there to enjoy the opening day of the display of pencil sketches and various other artworks, by a certain local artist named Ms. Ann Lolita.

The press releases and promotional events leading up to the actual opening of the display had been a rousing success. This long-awaited event of the unfolding of a lifetime of dreams, becoming a reality, had created quite a stir through the artistic communities of the city and beyond.

An elderly man walked up to and spoke to Ann while she stood on the sideline greeting people and watching the crowd.

"Congratulations, Ann. My goodness, what a wonderful and inspirational achievement this is for the gallery and for you. You must be so proud. I know I am! This is an even greater opening day turnout than I would ever have imagined. Some bids presented tonight for your artwork are almost unimaginable. People are bidding twenty percent over the listed prices." He was dressed in a fine suit, with a nametag on his lapel to show that he was the owner of the establishment. He shook Ann's hand while smiling broadly.

Ann stood there smiling and glowing, sipping from a glass of wine, dressed to the hilt in a fine dress, a simple gold chain hanging seductively around her neck.

She was looking as fine as fine could be. . ..

"Thank you, Mr. Jenkins. It is indeed a dream that has come true. I have you to thank, for believing in me, for giving me a chance."

The elderly man waved his hand in the air as if to discount Ann's statement.

"Nonsense, one look at your work, speaks for itself. You did this all yourself. I just gave you a vehicle to arrive in where you should have been a long time ago. In addition, you breathed new energy into my own life and in the center, too. For that, I thank you."

He turned and pointed towards a certain sketch hanging on the wall in front of them; a sketch that was the only piece in the entire gallery of which a small roped off area was set in front of in order to keep the many admirers and viewers at a safe distance from the hallowed artwork. A security guard stood in the corner near the drawing, keeping a close eye on the crowd and their behavior.

Numerous people stood around this particular drawing. More of the crowd was viewing this piece than any other work in the entire display.

"I sure do wish that people would stop placing bids on that sketch. It is making my heart race, the amount of money they keep offering. For an old man, such as I am, it is becoming a bit precarious. We keep telling everyone that the original is not for sale, they can purchase the reproductions, but the original of 'The Quiet Stranger in the Black Hat', is not for sale at any price."

Mr. Jenkins finished his statement, took a sip of his wine, looked over the rim of the glass, and studied Ann's face for a potential change of heart.

After all, he had a business to run.

"That is, in fact . . . still true . . . right, Ann?" Mr. Jenkins asked just to make sure.

Ann smiled and placed her hand on Mr. Jenkins' shoulder, while confirming the status of the work, "Oh yes, not for sale at any price. I am sorry. Please excuse me. I need to go outside for a smoke and to take a break."

Ann excused herself and she made her way through the crowd. Along the way, she stopped many times to chat with admirers congratulating her and making small talk. Her captivating appearance only promoted her work and her image, and helped to sell even more of her work today.

Ann finally reached the side door; she opened it and stepped outside onto a small porch. There she stood, in the cool, late afternoon air.

It was cold, but the air felt so good.

She reached into her purse, pulled out a cigarette, and while she searched for a lighter in the depths of her purse, she heard the loud, distinct click of a lighter from behind her.

She turned around in haste and looked straight into the eyes of the quiet stranger in the black hat. She was not surprised at his magical and sudden arrival because in her heart and in her soul; she somehow knew that he would be here today.

He held the flame out for Ann and under the dark brim of his hat; Ann could see him smile at her. She smiled back, leaned into the flame, and drew a strong pull on the cigarette to light it.

One long drag and a puff of smoke into the air.

"I wondered if I would ever see you again. I thought today would be as good a time as any for you to return. You do seem to have a knack for timing your arrival at just the right moment," Ann said, while looking deeply once again into those wonderfully haunting eyes.

He captivated her, whoever he was.

As usual, the quiet stranger did not say anything. He stood there in silence while studying her face as she puffed on the cigarette.

"I am not even going to try to surmise who you are, where you came from, or why. I think it is best at this point, just to hold you near and dear in my heart forever. I do not suppose that I could ask you to step inside, share a glass of wine with me, perhaps, even dinner and who knows what else later."

Ann smiled. She was embarrassed at her proposition, and she waved her hand in the air as if to suggest to the quiet stranger that he should forget the entire thought.

"Please, do not answer that one. I already know what you would say. Let me dream, please, let me dream of how wonderful that would be for me, or for us."

He nodded his head and smiled.

She took one last puff and tossed the half-smoked cigarette out into the street. She reached out her hands, and the quiet stranger took them into his hands. She once again felt that warmth; his spirit projected such warmth, even on a bitterly cold day.

"Thank you for giving me my life back. I did return every penny to Miss Wainwright and then I kicked that gambling maniac to the curb. I started to sketch again within hours after you left, but I know that you already know all of these facts."

He nodded, yet remained silent.

"I now know that I have recovered what was lost inside of me, and for that, I have to thank you again. You gave it back to me, quiet stranger."

Suddenly, she hit a nerve with the quiet stranger. Something that she had said had finally caused a reaction within him.

He shook his head gently back and forth and finally, he spoke, "No, my dear Ann. You are wrong, because it never left you. I cannot return what was never gone. You see, when we become lost in a wayward life, we sometimes think that we lose parts of us along the way. All we need to find it once again, is to take the time to examine our hearts and find the true answers. I did not do that for you, nor can I ever do that for anyone. Only you can search your own heart. All that I can do is to remind you to examine it. I help people to face the truth, of which they already know within their hearts. Now, please never lose your dreams again. To lose your own heart and your dreams is as if you have died inside. Never die inside again, dear Ann. You have too much love, beauty and talent to give to this tired, old world."

He pursed his lips together, touched his fingers to them, and then gently placed his fingers upon Ann's cheek. She reached up, held his hands tightly upon her cheek, and closed her eyes.

Always, Ann wanted to remember this moment and the feel of his hands upon her skin.

She finally, reluctantly, let him go. He stepped back, nodded, smiled, tipped his hat, turned and walked briskly away.

Ann whispered, "I promise that I will never let go of my dreams again, quiet stranger. I think forever more that you will haunt me and you will always be part of them, too. No matter where I go, what I do, or when I think—I will always bring you with me. Now, until the end of all time. Thank you."

She stood on the steps next to the front door; she stood there for a long time until she could no longer see him or hear the click of the metal tips of his boots on the sidewalk.

Except in her mind and in her heart, forever more.

THE END

As the Flame Flickers

It was a bustling New England tourist town. A town nestled in a hidden enclave, with a main street boasting a legendary and picturesque view of snow-capped mountains, surrounded with ski resorts. It was a magnet for tourists, a picture-perfect postcard town, all tucked within the valley of the White Mountains.

The magnificent scenery alone captured your mind's eye forever!

On a day blessed with clear and mild weather, the village green in the center of the town would fill with pencil sketching artists; oil and watercolor painters equipped with flowing palettes filled with colors, photographers armed with the latest in technology or just a point and shoot camera, all in pursuit of the perfect picture. There, they all would capture the backdrop scenes surrounding the town forever on their canvas, their sketching pads, or in full film or digital wonder.

It was an amazing place of natural beauty, a place full of vibrant life, yet it was somewhat full of quiet solitude, too.

The little town had it all. It had ski resorts, honeymoon retreats for lovers, breathtaking views of the Presidential Range of mountains, hiking, fishing, moose hunting, sightseeing, fine restaurants, arts and crafts from local artists; it was a haven of bliss!

Fergus Samuel Dempsey, or as everyone knew him better by his common term of endearment, "Sam" owned and operated a store, which was smack dab in the center of the main street of this town. For lack of a better description, it was a general store, but in reality, he sold a little bit of everything, "New England." It was without a doubt the typical tourist trap of retail lust for browsing shoppers wanting to bring back to their homes and memories, a piece of their holiday to this little piece of Heaven on Earth.

Sam Dempsey earned a nice living at this little store. He paid a handsome chunk of change to the landlord for the rent, but the location made it all worthwhile.

It was a gold mine.

Sam settled here from his native New Jersey many years ago. He had vacationed here often with his wife and his children, and they fell in love with the area and location.

What was there not to love about it?

It was just what they enjoyed for family getaways. It boasted not only breathtaking scenery but also had all the activities they enjoyed as a family. They all felt as if it was like no place on the face of the Earth. Skiing, ice skating, the great outdoors, hiking and fishing, the perfect outdoor adventure retreat! Over a period of years, after many family visits, they vowed, if they ever caught the fever of wanderlust and sought to find their own perfect haven of bliss; they would sell everything in New Jersey and escape to the White Mountains.

Together, they would start their lives over here, away from the madness of the hustle and bustle of their busy New Jersey lifestyles. Away from high taxes, endless traffic jams, irate people, jobs that require long hours with no clear rewards, and all the confusion that living in New Jersey requires.

Their dream came to fruition a little sooner than they imagined.

After reaching the thirty-year mark working in an executive position with a worldwide corporation, Sam recognized all the obvious warning signs of the proverbial "end of the road" coming for him at his place of employment.

First, Sam's longtime boss rather reluctantly, "retired." Madness ensued, with endless and mindless shuffling of the corporate structure. He then reported to a department head, who knew nothing as to what duties Sam actually performed on a day-to-day basis. Sam had been around long enough to know that this was always a bad sign, when your position was no longer relevant enough for someone to know, or even care, what you did for the company.

Corporate mergers were imminent, changes on the horizon, executives forced to retire, severance pay, all the typical American corporate madness!

He held on for one more year before the train finally pulled into the station for the last run.

After thirty-one years of fighting the war, Sam took the retirement package and their generous offer and ran so far away that he was just dust in the wind. Since their children had all grown up and moved away, Sam and his wife finally made their dream come to fruition. His wife also retired from her position and they sold it all, their house, land, cars, trucks, took his pension and her savings, and together, they lived their dream and fled from the congestion of New Jersey, to the solitude of the White Mountains.

The Dempsey's bought their dream house. It was a log cabin, three bedrooms, a sleeping loft, open floor plan on the first floor, with a custom kitchen. The feature that Sam and his wife enjoyed the most was that on the first floor, it boasted a floor to ceiling window that looked out on their backyard. A backyard, which was snuggled into the side of a mountain. Through the window was a breathtaking view for Sam and his wife to enjoy, all while they sat in front of their fireplace sipping red wine. All of this, yet, they were close to the town and all the amenities, too. They could arrive at the local food store in less than ten minutes.

It was amazing, but they were finally living their dream.

There was only one trouble left now. What would they do? You can only sip so much wine, stare out so many windows and both Sam and his wife, were both still young with the both of them, still in their early fifties. They could easily work another twenty years. Money was not actually an issue. He had his lucrative pension, and his wife had a nice retirement too from her job. It was not money, but instead, it was a bit of yearning for more challenges that they shared. They both were energetic, vigorous and ambitious people, and they agreed that they both needed to stay active in their minds and bodies.

Since they decided that it was too early to pack it all in and fish, ski, sightsee and hike every day, Sam and his wife joined up with a number of local charity organizations, as well as local hobby clubs and other social interactions. There, they met people and mingled in with the locals in the community. Sam and his wife were both dynamic personalities, attractive looking, in good physical condition, and they were great conversationalists. They attracted people naturally and made friends easily.

Sam and his wife both always enjoyed photography and with all the fantastic scenery that abounded in the area and living within this gorgeous mountain valley, they now had a tremendous opportunity for snapping landscape scenery pictures. With this pursuit in mind, the couple signed up with a local cultural arts center that offered photography classes.

The instructor of the course was an elderly gentleman, an avid camera buff and a longtime resident of the town. He was a kind man, very patient and extremely gifted at photography. The entire class of students marveled at his skills, since it was easy to see that most of his pictures were akin to a professional level. His skill with a camera was much more than just a casual amateur photographer's skill would be and certainly, leaps and bounds beyond the skills of an amateur who might, on rare occasion, get lucky with a nice shot or two.

Sam and his wife began a friendship with the instructor. The relationship began around cameras, taking photos in the field, learning in the classroom, a budding friendship centered on their mutual hobby, but it ultimately led to a business deal.

The gentleman owned a small general store in the center of town, a lucrative retail operation, and he told Mr. and Mrs. Dempsey that he was thinking of selling the establishment and joining his children in Florida. His wife had passed on a few years earlier and despite his community activities, teaching photography, and running the store, he sorely missed his family. They were pressuring him to sell the business and come to live near them. He had no family close by and he humbly confessed to his friends how difficult and lonely life had become for him since his wife had passed.

Loneliness is a pain few people can evade or tolerate for very long. Of all the emotional pains, loneliness might be the harshest of them all; it slowly eats away at your soul and erodes your mind.

The elderly gentleman felt that Sam and his wife were the perfect couple to buy his store and run the operation. In the Dempsey's, he saw the perfect combinations of skills and attributes with big-city smarts; they were both skilled with business poise and shrewdness, both attractive people who could mingle with customers, and he was confident that they would be successful at retail sales. After many long discussions and more than a bit of gentle arm-twisting, Sam and his wife agreed.

The elderly gentleman was indeed correct with his judgement because the Dempsey's bought the store and turned a successful business into an even more successful business.

For two years, it was pure magic.

The Dempsey's were now living the dream, enjoying life, running a successful local business and becoming an integral part of the community. They grew into highly respected leaders, highly engaged and involved in local civic organizations, different types of charities, retail promotional organizations, and together, they volunteered for countless nonprofit events and fundraisers.

It was a dream come true.

Until it all collapsed.

It started with his wife just not feeling her normal, energetic self. Maybe she was doing too much. Everyone told her to take a few weeks off, relax, visit the children, calm down a little, and surely, she would rebound.

She did not rebound and finally, when she began to feel progressively worse, she went to the doctor for a full examination.

It was not good news.

A disease, a wretched, progressive, horrible disease. More tests, more treatments, endless trips downstate to the more advanced hospitals in Nashua and in Manchester, then on to the world-renowned hospitals in Boston.

As often occurs with these horrid diseases, they tease you into thinking a recovery is in the works; it is a cruel manner in which they operate. Sam's wife, despite the dim future and prognosis predicted by the teams of doctors, did begin to feel better.

Then, she suddenly went downhill quite quickly.

Life is at times so full of joy, so full of love and hope, and then it has the dark side. The wretched, cold, evil side, which no one ever wants to face, but we all have eventually to encounter, while we pass through the seasons of our lives. The lesson is always to make each day count, each moment, every second, because all too soon, it all is gone. . ..

Sam's wife passed on after a long fight, a valiant and brave fight with a cruel, heartless enemy. She lived a wonderful life, a loving person whose life ended all too early.

Tragedy comes in many varieties and it is a painful aspect of this life on Earth.

She left her husband crushed, defeated, his spirit stolen, his heart broken, her children, grandchildren, and friends in shambles.

Yet Sam trudged on, never quite as happy, never quite as motivated as he had been, but he vowed to continue with their dream. When Sam's wife knew that the fight was lost, when she felt the pending sunset on her horizon, his wife had made Sam make a solemn promise to her. She made Sam vow to live his life to the fullest, find someone to share his love with and, most importantly, never to cave into the gloom. He would not break that promise, no matter how difficult it proved to be. He did his best never to forget, yet to move on with his life.

Each day was a struggle, each day was another obstacle. Happiness escaped him and now loneliness crept into his soul too.

About one year or so after his wife passed away, on a cold, snowy, slightly gloomy, late January day, Sam manned the store. He had his part-time help working with him, with two young people who helped him with general duties, stocking shelves, ringing up sales, all kinds of daily chores. They were good workers, reliable and friendly too and he appreciated not only their efforts but also their company.

On this day, Sam sat alone in his office, in front of his desk, he was working on some bookkeeping; the store was usually quiet on days such as this one was. The snow was falling hard outside; its happy arrival had sent droves of tourists, as well as residents, to the ski slopes. Business would pick up later, when the folks left the slopes and wandered into town for dining, or for some sight-seeing and store browsing.

The snow was a welcome visitor here in New Hampshire; it was a part of the mystique, part of the magic, white gold for the ski resorts and it added to the New England experience. The town's maintenance workers did not even bother plowing the main road until it was too deep for safe passage, and even then, they left enough of a coating for the horse-drawn sleighs of the local resort to glide upon, while they went up and down the road carrying happy visitors.

Sam loved snapping pictures of tourists from Florida, or other tropical climates that stopped by his store. The people who had never seen snow before were extra special and lots of fun, too. He would happily snap their pictures, the folks smiling in his store with the snow experience as a backdrop. It was a part of his business, in which he truly cherished.

Sam had good days and, of course, his bad days too.

When it was quiet, it was the worst of times for Sam. Today was one of those days. While he sat at his desk, his mind wandered. He found it hard to focus, hard to forget, and for some reason, visions of yesteryears wove in and out of his mind. His wife, his children, his time at the corporation, slugging it out day after day with mind-numbing corporate madness. How he wished he had moved to this area sooner. If he had done so, perhaps, he could have more of the happy moments to remember, rather than the troubled ones.

Nowadays, he felt as if he had very few of the happier moments to remember. For some reason, they now buried deep in his mind and they were becoming harder and harder for him to recall. He felt pain; he felt loneliness, both time and happiness, all stolen from him all too soon.

All stolen, in some type of cruel manner.

He thought how it was so strange now, after all of these years, that he still rarely, if ever, told people his actual first name. It was not that Fergus was such a bad name or was a name that he despised or thought was so terrible; it was that he felt as if Sam suited him so much better.

He, of course, used his legal name on required documents or in certain transactions, but very few, if any, folks around here would know who Fergus Samuel Dempsey was! There was, however, someone a long time ago, who despite his best efforts to hide his name and use Sam as his main title of address, steadfastly refused to call him by anything but his real name. She was so stubborn, and my goodness, she was so beautiful too! While Sam sat there, he suddenly remembered this beautiful woman, who insisted upon calling him Fergus in a gentle, soft voice.

A woman, who at one time, a very long time ago, was very important to him in his life.

He did not know why his mind wandered so much today or why this special woman from his long, lost past suddenly and inexplicably returned to his thoughts. A woman, whom he never told his wife about, not for any particular reason, other than to hold this special woman forever more in a coveted place in his heart.

He was sometimes ashamed to admit to anyone other than his own heart that this special woman brought Fergus to a place of which he had never been before. To a plane higher than he ever dreamed could exist. A place of which he never returned to, not even in the arms of his beloved wife.

It was his special secret.

It was his special chance at that once in a lifetime love that very few people could ever enjoy in their lifetimes. Of all times, why now did he hear her voice suddenly calling his name from deep in the past?

Why today? What had changed?

Strange, very strange. . ..

Sam met her five or so years before he had met his wife, during that magical time, when you were so young, so innocent, so wide open for all of life's passions and adventures.

They met in the early autumn, on a golden day, full of pure sunshine, colored leaves and blue skies. Sam was around twenty years of age and she was a few years older. Sam fell for her so deeply that even now when he recalled the moment when they first met; his heartbeat increased just thinking about that special moment.

Paige was her first name; Paige Ippolito was her full name. She was of Italian-American descent, and she was a woman of rare and intoxicating beauty. Sultry, alluring, with dark and deep-set eyes, long black hair, a smile that melted men's hearts, and she spoke in a soft, yet captivating voice. Paige carried herself so confidently that every man, who came into her presence, fell in love with her at first sight.

Of all the men who followed her around, she picked Sam. Not that it was so much of a stretch, because Sam was not exactly a slouch in the looks and personality department either, and he did have quite the selection of the young ladies pursuing him, it was just that Paige was creative and she had a light, breezy and somewhat, liberal personality. Whereas Sam was ultraconservative, well-grounded and always logical.

Sam and Paige shared some classes of studies in college; she was a budding journalist; he was a business major, and when their paths crossed, there was some type of magic, some type of connection.

Love follows no clear-cut, actual rules, nor does it often respect many boundaries. It is another strange but wonderful aspect of this magical world.

Soon, they were deeply in love and the passion in which they shared; Sam could never duplicate again in his life.

Ever.

While he sat back in his chair, his eyes wandered to the ceiling, and he exhaled deeply.

He could see Paige standing there in front of him,

smiling, with her radiant face glowing, her soft voice telling him, "Fergus, we are soul mates. You and I are forever. We will always link together as one. You need to realize that soul mates are one for life. People are sometimes lucky enough to have more than one, but the bonds they forge, the chains they create, link by link, inch by inch, never can be broken. Often, in love, it is a universal season for people such as we are. Time passes but our love remains."

Sam shook off the vision; it was too powerful, too emotional, and too full of wonderment for him to think about for very long.

Paige's career ambitions and dreams were to be a serious news journalist, but in her spare time, she also wrote. She wrote novels, some short stories, as well as poems and song lyrics for her musician friends.

Sam often felt that was her true calling, a calling, which she needed to pursue, but Paige dabbled at it more as if it was a hobby. Everyone that she shared her writings with felt the same as Sam did, but she would laugh at their encouragement and dismiss any thoughts of a silly career writing some words on a paper.

A specific memory flashed into Fergus Samuel Dempsey's mind. A fond memory, but it was certainly a painful one too, and it was a nagging one.

Sam opened his desk drawer. He reached deep into the confines, dug around and pulled out a small booklet. A journal of notes with all of them held together with an old rubber band. A well-worn book, which without the assistance of the band, might crumble into a pile of dusty memories and be swept up and lost forever in the passages of time. Sam had changed the rubber bands to fresh ones a number of times over the years.

However, Sam would never let that happen because this book, well, it contained parts of his life. Newspaper clippings, pictures of his wife, printed memories and scraps of his family, notes of his own, birth announcements clipped out of newspapers, as well as sad obituaries of loved ones and friends who passed away. It was all here, the annals and records of his life.

It also contained a special piece of paper. A paper, in which Sam, for an unknown reason, needed to find and to read, on this snowy, January day.

Towards the back of the book, he found it and when he did, he carefully unfolded it and read the words of a poem aloud. A poem in which Paige had written upon the paper long ago, but for some reason, she never finished. . ..

"As the flame flickers, so goes our lives.
Bright at first, then often flickering and dancing.
Dancing in time with the ebb and the flow,
until it dies.

As the flame flickers, so goes our minds.
Bright at first, then often dull with pain.
Dancing in time with the ebb and the flow,
until it dies.

As the flame flickers, so goes our hearts.
Beating together as if we were one.
Dancing in time, with the ebb and the flow,
until it dies.

As the flame flickers, so goes our love.
More powerful than our own souls.
Dancing in time with the ebb and the flow.
However, our love never dies."

Sam stopped reading; he folded the paper carefully and placed it back inside the journal. He pushed back a tear while the memory he never wanted to revisit returned to him. A memory, which duplicated the classic movie-scene, the tearful, horrible, lost, love scene. It unraveled in his mind and he recalled Paige holding his hands, telling him of her plans to leave New Jersey, her plans to attend a university in Northern California. How much she loved him, but she had to leave. They would always be together in their hearts and minds . . . all the usual dialogue that seemed as if it was right out of the script of a tearjerker movie.

It was, of course, the last time Sam ever saw or heard from her. Love lost—the tie that bound them, cast to the flickering flame in her poem. Emotional pain, crushed hearts, terrible heartbreak. All he had left was a dusty book with a crumbling rubber band to hold the memories together.

He never got over her, ever.

The classic movie scene, recreated in real life.

Two years later, Sam met his wife and Paige's quite prophetic words of how some people have more than one soul mate in this world—came to be true.

Now, all these years later, alone in his love life, his wife long since passed on, Sam could not help but wonder where Paige was. Why are these thoughts occurring today? Why, after all of these years? He could not shake the thoughts; it was all a little strange. Did she marry? Did she have children? What became of their chain? Did the flame ever really flicker and go out?

Noontime came and Sam's store clerks took their lunch breaks. He would cover the store's sales floor for an hour or so, and with the snow coming down so hard, Sam knew that it would be quiet until later in the day. As he often did, for the afternoon rush, Sam went around the store and he took a match to a few of the scented candles scattered about the store. The lure of the scents of the classic products created right here in New England would entice a few sales when the crowds came in later in the day.

He also lit the fancy oil lamp set on the front counter. A

lamp that had turned out to be one of his best-selling pieces of merchandise. After Sam lit the flame, he turned the wick down, so the flame just barely illuminated within the glass chimney. The glass created a prism of colors that projected on the countertop and the ceiling of the store, while surrounding the flame with a soft glow. Sam knew all the retail tricks and the oil lamps sold so well that he oftentimes could not even resupply them fast enough. Sam rather fancied that part of the huge sales of the oil lamps were because of his efforts at marketing.

He now stood behind the front counter, glancing through register sales, when suddenly the flame in the oil lamp blew out in front of him. Then he watched while all the flames of the candles that he had just lit . . . one by one, all of them also extinguished. All of them went out together, as if a wild rush of wind, or some type of draft, blew around his store and sucked the flames out of their confines.

It was indeed quite strange; the door had not opened, the furnace heat had not turned on, the back door for deliveries was still intact. Where did this draft come from? Sam stood there puzzled, because there had been no draft or wind. What caused all the flames to flicker and then extinguish so mysteriously?

Sam reached for the oil lamp glass when the door to the store opened, and through it walked a very tall, lean, but powerful looking man. Sam watched as he moved quickly in from the snowfall, and he immediately noticed his unusual appearance. This was a large man, wearing a black, wide-brimmed hat, dressed sharply in expensive looking clothes. He wore sharply creased black trousers; a black shirt tucked neatly under a black leather vest. A vest was all this man wore to combat the snow, wind, and cold. He did not wear an overcoat, only a black leather vest unbuttoned, except for the last button in the row.

While studying the stranger, Sam could not help but

think that although his clothes seemed so expensive and brand new, he appeared as if he was from the past or from some bygone era in time.

Sam watched as the man dressed in black stopped walking a few feet into the entrance of the store. He turned, and looked around, as if he was finding his bearings of some sort.

The man then identified something of interest; Sam could see his eyes move towards a display in the rear of the store.

Mr. Dempsey watched while the man walked briskly over to a display of pictures and a rack of postcards mounted on a wall in the rear of the store. It was then that Sam noticed the highly polished boots on his feet. Boots with metal tips that made a distinct clicking noise as the man moved across the wooden floor of the store. Boots that had no disturbances upon their finish, not even the slightest blemish, or any sign of snow or ice, despite the weather in which the man in black had just removed himself from, when he came into the store. Sam scanned the man again, and it was then, when his eyes moved from the boots to the wide-brimmed hat he wore on his head, that Sam noticed his hat did not have a trace of snow on it either!

The man carried with him an ominous presence of some sort. Sam could not help but to feel it, but he shook it off rather quickly. After all, a customer is a customer.

"Welcome to the Nook of New Hampshire! Bet you are glad to be out of that snow and ice," Sam shouted out to the man, as he relit the oil lamp on the counter.

The man did not answer him, or even look his way, but Sam watched as the man in black continued browsing the display of postcards and photographs. Sam moved from behind the counter and he worked his way through the store towards the candles, stopping at each one and relighting the flames as he went along.

"Feel free to browse around. We have a bit of everything here. Some of those photographs there on the display in front of you, I took myself right here on Main Street in town, or the former owner of the store took, or my wife. . . ."

Sam's voice drifted off when he started to mention his wife. He could not finish the sentence.

It was then that he noticed the man in black turn around and he looked directly and deeply into Sam's eyes. Their eyes met in a fleeting, yet somewhat ominous moment. It was then; in which Sam saw, close up, a handsome man, a man with a close-trimmed beard and facial hair neat as a pin, not a single hair out of place and dark, black, piercing eyes that looked directly into Sam's soul.

Now, for a reason that he was not too sure of, he was very nervous. Sam held onto the counter where the candle sat and his hands shook, while he moved his eyes from the man in black, back to the candle. He steadied himself in an effort to relight the wick.

The man in black said not a single word, but Sam could feel his eyes studying him, while Sam struggled to relight the candle.

Sam thought to himself, "Who the hell is this quiet stranger in a black hat? Why did his eyes just pierce my heart and send shivers up and down my spine?" Sam recovered, lit the candle and moved on in order to light the next candle.

He tried once again to invoke a response from the quiet stranger, "I have not seen you in here or around town before. You must be visiting or passing through, huh? Are you a tourist? I would think if you spend any time outside today that you might want to pick up a winter coat. Wearing that thin vest and just a hat, might not cut it around here with this stretch of weather we are having."

In an effort to break the ice, Sam smiled and laughed a bit, but the quiet stranger ignored him and continued to poke around the rack of postcards. The quiet stranger did not even lift his head or his eyes to acknowledge the conversation.

Sam lit the last of the candles and for just a few seconds, he studied the quiet stranger. He decided to give up on conversation and return to the front counter, to wait and see what, if anything, that the quiet stranger in the black hat would choose to purchase.

The storekeeper returned to studying his register sales slips and when he once again heard the metal tips of the quiet stranger's boots moving along the floor, he looked up to see the stranger moving towards him. Sam saw that in his hand. He held a single postcard. Sam smiled as the quiet stranger reached the counter and set the postcard upon the counter while reaching inside one of his vest pockets. He could not help but admire the way the man was dressed, his immaculate clothes and, despite the perceived ominous presence, those dark eyes. . ..

"Well now, a postcard, a memento of your visit here," Sam said, while he reached for the card to check for a price and ring up the meager sale.

To the storekeeper's shock, the quiet stranger finally spoke, and he spoke in a low, deep, yet melodious voice, as he softly said, "Not really, not of a visit to this town at least. It might be a link to your past, but not to mine."

The words were puzzling, and Sam looked at the quiet stranger and watched as he first moved his dark eyes from Sam's eyes and face, then back to the postcard sitting upon the counter. The quiet stranger pointed at the postcard with his finger, as if to prompt Sam to study it closer.

With a nod of his head, Sam agreed, and he looked at the front of the postcard, and a cold shiver went down his spine, because he saw it was a postcard of a landscape scene labeled in bold letters, "Redwood City, California, U.S.A."

His hands shook while he studied the card. He looked at

the quiet stranger and he theorized that this was some type of error.

"Why, this is a mistake. I am very sorry, sir. This must be an error of some sort. My clerks must have made a stocking mistake, or it was an error in shipment from my supplier and we did not catch it. You see, we do not sell postcards of locations in California here in my store."

Sam's voice drifted off when he saw the quiet stranger's face break into a slight smile and the stranger began, rather slowly, to shake his head as if to disagree with Sam's statement.

The quiet stranger in the black hat spoke again, "No, there is no error. I disagree. You will sell one now. Please read the back of the postcard too. I would recommend you check into Redwood City. The weather is a bit better than it is here right now. I also know that soul mates are one for life. Certain special people in this world are sometimes lucky enough to have more than one, but the bonds they forge, the chains they create, link by link, inch by inch, never can be broken. Oftentimes, in love, there are universal seasons for people such as you are Fergus. Time passes, but your love remains."

The quiet stranger in the black hat tugged at the brim of his hat, pulling it down some over his face, as if to somewhat shield his facial features from Sam's view.

He then spoke very softly, kindly and gently as he said, "These feelings that you have had today, these trips to the past, they are for a reason, Fergus. Do not ignore your heart because, I think that it might be time for her to complete the last verse of the poem."

While dumbfounded, Sam stood there. He was still too stunned to decide if this was a dream, a faded memory, or some type of hallucination! The quiet stranger even knew his actual name.

How the hell?

The quiet stranger in the black hat dropped five dollars

in single bills upon the counter. He looked at the befuddled storekeeper one last time, smiled, tipped his hat and turned briskly towards the door.

Fergus Samuel Dempsey was too bewildered to say a word.

It seemed as if all the bones in his body shook and rattled with the very words in which the quiet stranger had just spoken to him. He held on for dear life to the edge of the sales counter, and before he could recover, the stranger had reached the door, opened it and disappeared into the weather.

As Sam's hands trembled, he slowly turned the postcard over in his hands and with all the courage in which he could muster, he read aloud the back of the card, "Redwood City, California, where all the flames might flicker, but they never extinguish."

When he finished speaking the words, all the candles in the store, once again, went out, but the oil lamp's flame flickered, yet it remained lit. It struggled, and then it danced around the wick a little, ebbed and then recovered. It then burned high, it burned bright and strong in front of him, and the smoke from the wick slowly drifted out of the glass chimney.

Sam watched as the wisps of smoke slowly drifted away.

Three months later, Fergus Samuel Dempsey slowly walked through an international airport in Northern California. He waded through the waves and waves of humanity and made his way from his arrival gate to the terminal . . . when their eyes met once again.

He had suddenly appeared, mysteriously, out of masses of nameless faces of humans rushing along.

There he was, the quiet stranger in the black hat.

Sam saw him standing along a wall, waiting and watching.

Sam's face broke into a smile. He peeled out of the

crowd and he walked over to where the quiet stranger in the black hat stood.

He stood next to him, smiled, and before he could reach out to offer to shake his hand, the quiet stranger put his hand on Sam's shoulder and smiled too. Sam met those dark, piercing eyes once again. Yet, on this go around; they did not seem quite so ominous.

This time, they filled with a warm glow.

Sam spoke softly, "Once I recovered from shock and composed myself, I found Paige on the internet that same afternoon that you left me the clue. I wrote to her the next day. She answered right away."

The emotions caused him to stop, then after a slight pause as Sam gathered his thoughts, he began speaking again.

"Somehow, I knew you would be here today and somehow, I know that you already know all of this of which I am telling you. I guess I still want to tell you though, you know, in order to confirm all of this in my own mind. To make sure that this is not some type of crazy hallucination."

Sam held his palms gently on his head, and then he shook his head as if to test to see if he was dreaming. He then explained, "Her husband had passed suddenly too, just a few months before my. . .."

The quiet stranger tightened his grip on Sam's shoulder as if to comfort him when he stumbled on the words and the memory.

The quiet stranger did not say a word, but he remained smiling widely at him and he listened carefully and thoughtfully, while Sam regained his composure and spoke again, "Geez, this wild world is filled with such mysteries. I cannot begin to tell you how I have struggled with all of this, all that has happened, why it did, what it is all about. All I know is that we found one another again. We found each other, even after all of these years, all the heartaches that we went through both individually, and I guess in some way, collectively too."

Sam looked away for a moment, breathed deeply, and continued speaking with a wide smile upon his face. He realized that this was all real and that he was not dreaming.

"It is all so amazing, but I am not going to argue with the results! I will never try to figure out who you are, where you came from, and why, but I want to thank you. Paige is waiting for me right now on the other side of the terminal here, and I bet you know this too, but she told me on the telephone before I left New Hampshire that she finally finished the poem."

The quiet stranger did not speak, but instead, he nodded his head to confirm that he did indeed already know that.

"I guess you relight the flames that go out in this world. Is that your ultimate mission here in this world, dark, quiet stranger? To reignite the flames which flicker within our lives?"

The quiet stranger in the black hat dropped his hand from Sam's shoulder, stepped backwards and leaned forward, while he adjusted the brim of his hat to look at him through the top of his eyes.

He finally spoke, "No Fergus, those kinds of flames never extinguish, ever, not the kind you share with Paige. All I do is to make sure that people such as you are, people who long ago, for whatever reason, lost the view of the flame, find their way back to it. The flame flickered. But fate would never allow it to go out. It never will, Fergus. Not now, not until the end of all time."

The quiet stranger in the black hat stepped back, nodded, smiled, tipped his hat, turned and walked briskly away.

Fergus Samuel Dempsey stood there for a long time, watching as he made his way through the mass of human traffic in the airport and until he could no longer hear the click of the metal tips of his boot upon the walkway.

Twenty minutes later, two long lost lovers embraced, amongst tears of reunion joy and within flames burning bright and strong. While they shared a kiss, Paige silently tucked a note inside of Fergus' shirt pocket.

The note contained the poem. The poem was now finally complete, with the final verse written upon it.

A poem that took a long time to finish, but a poem that was worth waiting for, despite the universal seasons that needed to pass through two special lives. Until now, the final verse was unable to be completed, or even thought of, because the final verse was still yet to arrive. . ..

As the Flame Flickers

As the flame flickers, so goes our lives.
Bright at first, then often flickering and dancing.
Dancing in time, with the ebb and the flow,
until it dies.

As the flame flickers, so goes our minds.
Bright at first, then often dull with pain.
Dancing in time with the ebb and the flow,
until it dies.

As the flame flickers, so goes our hearts.
Beating together as if we were one.
Dancing in time, with the ebb and the flow,
until it dies.

As the flame flickers, so goes our love.
More powerful than our own souls.
Dancing in time with the ebb and the flow.
However, our love never dies.

As the flame flickers, then expires, it drifts off into smoke.

Dancing in time with the ebb and the flow.
Smoke that holds memories, words, love, holds pain, and it holds joy.
It drifts off, never to be seen again, rising, twirling, slowly, moving out of our sight.

Even when you think that, the flame has finally expired, the flame never really dies.
Somewhere, the flame burns forever.
On and on it burns, dances, ebbs and flows.
Now and forever until the end of all time.

As the flame flickers, so goes our love.
On and on until the end of all time.

THE END

Dust of the Ages

She sat on the train in the early morning hours, staring blankly out the smutty window while riding into the big city, watching the endless trees, poles, signs, billboards, and boring snow-covered landscape as it all flew by her window. It always looked the same.

Rat-at-tat-tat, the wheels of the train lulled you into complacency.

A typical weekday for the infinite commuter where nothing much ever changes.

One after another, the scenes and days blended into one another and it all looked and often felt the same.

It was late January, and New Jersey currently suffered within the grasp of a harsh winter that seemed as if the warm autumn of the past year was an ancient memory. Yet, somewhere on the horizon, a promise of spring loomed on a bleak horizon. It seemed as if it would never arrive.

The young woman shifted uneasily on the hard seat of the train. She laughed a little at the thought of how joyful the first snowfall in November could be, while covering the dull, dirty, urban landscape in a fresh white coat of beauty. Christmas comes and Christmas goes, and soon, by the time the end of January rolls around, everyone has grown weary of the fresh coats of white beauty.

She had been on her own for a long time now. She left home right after high school, off to her university studies, eager to escape her parent's tutelage and strike out on her own.

You know, she was ready to take the world over.

She was young, beautiful; no, correction, she was gorgeous. She was educated at some of the best schools, smart, and professional, and on her way up the ladder rungs in the company of her current employment.

A rising starlet.

She disliked the commute, but the wonderful salary and the marvelous opportunity, all combined to offset the long hours of rolling endlessly down the tracks.

She had grown tired of the music she had loaded upon her MP3 player and made a mental note to change it up in the near future. Pulling the ear buds out of her ears, she mindlessly picked up a book out of the bag at her feet. She was an avid reader, which was a trait she must have inherited from her father. Her father read and to the best of her knowledge, he still reads endlessly. While she fingered the pages of the book in her hand, she could hear him telling her how reading was the way in which he had taught himself. More so than any school he ever attended, he learned by reading.

This book was a paperback, written by a popular author. A book, which currently set the bestseller list on fire. Yet, as much as she tried to get into the author's writings, she could not. There was something missing. It was just another thriller with typical twists and turns and the outcome of the story mired in supposed, dark shadows. She knew better, because from the very first chapter, she knew how the story would turn out. She often wondered who pays off these so-called critics, to give such glowing reviews to the same old type of work.

She put the book back in her bag and continued to stare out the window. She disagreed with the glowing reviews of the author's works. It all seemed so commonplace, so stereotypical of everything else she read as of late.

Yet, what were the other choices?

Okay, let's see . . . zombies, violence, spies, subterfuge, the end of the world, or some sappy, horrible romance novel. No, she needed to find something else to pass the endless hours of boredom with while riding on this train.

She vowed to do it or to find a job in New Jersey closer to her home and forego the long ride into the city every day.

Her mind reverted in time to her family, her brother, her childhood growing up in New Jersey.

She loved New Jersey, despite the jokes and criticism it received. She remained a "Jersey Girl," and she was proud of it too. After happily leaving New Jersey to attend university out of state, she returned, realizing that there is no Isle of Avalon out there and New Jersey was *her* home.

It was where her memories were born and, in some cases, where they buried them too.

She knew it was part of her inner soul and she would never leave it ever again. She cheered for the local New York and New Jersey sports teams; she loved the culture, the accents, the entertainment, and she proudly ordered "cawwfeee" in the morning from youse guys and walked her "dawwwg" every day.

She stirred again in her seat and glanced at her watch. She still had another half an hour or so of this maddening train ride and upon seeing the time, she sighed deeply.

Her sigh caught the attention of the young man who always sat across the row from her. She could see him study her out of the corner of his eye. He was attractive, neat, clean-cut and well-dressed, even on Fridays. The young man seemed as if he was a young executive or a professional, in whatever his career position was. The young woman remained skeptical; when you looked as captivating as she did, these drooling hounds of testosterone were a plague. She knew that outward appearances meant zero, zilch, nothing.

She generally sat in the same location on the train and

no matter where she decided to sit, the young man always made his best effort to sit opposite her. She felt that the interactive cat-and-mouse game was actually somewhat cute on his part. He made conversation at every opportunity and raised his eyes to her whenever he could, in a vain effort to get to know the young woman. She had no intention of giving him the time of day or misleading him. Her career was of the most importance to her right now. She had no time for young men and their usual "ambitions."

As her mind wandered, she suddenly felt those familiar pangs of sorrow from her life today, combined with the wonderful memories of her childhood.

A strange combination, indeed.

Yes, she had a great many wonderful things in her life right now. She earned a large salary; she had professional status, an outstanding education, and fine clothes and a fancy apartment in Bergen County, New Jersey.

Yet deep down, she knew something was missing.

The feelings went deep, deeper than she ever wanted to admit. They stemmed from her estrangement from her father. The two of them had been so close when she was young; she often wondered where they drifted apart. Growing up, she shared all the love and joy that a child could have ever wanted or desired. She lived in warm houses, ate good food, as a youngster she had toys and gifts, profound love, a shoulder to lean and cry upon and enjoyed a rather carefree lifestyle.

The family vacationed here and there and she was always warm, dry and well fed! Her father was the sole provider for the family; he worked endless hours and paid for her university education as well as her brother's education, too. She squirmed a bit at the thought of the actual burden that must have placed upon him in this troublesome and expensive day and age.

Her childhood was happy. The joy continued all the way

to high school and then for a reason that she could not really pinpoint—they had grown divided.

Her father was an exceptional man, devoted to hard work, supporting his family, yet for some reason, she felt that he did not support her emotionally. He did not care or agree with her ambitions to travel out of state and follow her dreams. They never had shared a cruel word. He was not a stern or a harsh man. In fact, he was gentle and easygoing in many ways, but he did have strong convictions and opinions.

She felt because of his strong opinions that he had grown distant in his feelings toward her. He somewhat harshly predicted to her one day in an intense discussion that she would someday return to New Jersey, it was a part of her; she would never leave it for too long. She disagreed, the world had so much to offer; it was wide, exciting and an open palette to paint upon to her.

New Jersey! Hah! Gritty, urban, boring, unexciting. . ..

Then, as her father predicted, and she was somewhat embarrassed to admit, after all those travels, all those people, all the lure and scent of adventure, she was right back again in New Jersey.

After those years passed away, her father and she exchanged letters, Christmas cards and greetings via birthday cards, but she had not seen him face-to-face, or spoken to him personally in many years.

She could not actually answer why that was the case.

Perhaps she never did want to admit that he was in many ways correct in his opinions.

She reached down in her bag and pulled the paperback out again. She pulled her bookmark out from where she had just placed it and thought about how she needed to try the words once again. Perhaps reading again would stop her mind from wandering.

Perhaps.

A few lines, yes, yes, and no. Her mind could not focus.

She closed the book again and realized that the book reminded her of her father. You see, later on in his life, he had become a writer. He wrote in his spare time even though he had a full-time job too. Her father was a driven man, who was full of energy and zeal. Her father always had a mission.

His energy was boundless, and she realized that writing must be his release, a place for him to visit and keep his fertile mind occupied.

He wrote an awful lot. In fact, it was astounding the amount of material in which he wrote and produced. He wrote novels, short stories, novelettes, novellas, short articles, and random thoughts. His work consisted of mostly his own memories, his own adventures, stories of his own life of growing up in New Jersey. Her father wrote of his adventures with his lifelong best friend, he told tales of his past; he created new characters based upon actual folks that touched his life; he had hundreds of them and his books were very good. Or so she had heard.

You see, she never read one of his works.

Her father's mind was quite sharp and vivid. She always felt that she had inherited a good bit of his intelligence. She had read the reviews of his books. There were not many, but the ones that she could find praised his work as simple storytelling. That is something that seems as if it were a lost art these days.

The young woman read in the critical reviews of his work how he wrote of the pain of his life, the raw emotions combined with the joy of life, his loves, his victories and his defeats. She surmised how he expertly hid himself within his unique sense of humor, under the disguise of a fictional work; however, she knew him well enough to decipher it all.

She knew his eccentric ways and his vivid mind so well. He claimed that it was all pure fiction, but she knew there was much more fact to his volumes of writings than there was pure fiction.

By reading all the many actual descriptions of his published work, she could easily convince any slight remnant of her curiosity that none of his books would have any appeal to her. Without even glancing at a single word that her father wrote; she already knew that reading it all would be so matter of fact. It was all boring, humorous fiction with no zombies, no violence, no murders, and no end of the world plots. It was pure Americana, with a New Jersey twist.

It was easy for her to say that it was not her style and apparently, not really a popular style either for many other current and modern readers.

Her father never had a best seller.

Still, her father wrote on, and while she said it was not her style, she was slightly embarrassed to admit that it was wrong for her to say or think that when she had never read a single word of what he wrote.

Her own father's work and she never even opened a single page.

He had sent her many of his books; she had them all in a dusty collection, stuck in a box, a box hidden in a closet in her apartment. It seemed very profound to call her father's works a dusty collection. A collection, in which she never opened or even glanced at, or until now, had given them a second thought. The books sat there, unread, in an old box, collecting dust.

Dust of the ages.

She heard a noise and looked up to see where the noise had come from.

It was then that she saw him coming.

He was very lean, powerfully built and quite tall, so he took long strides, and he covered distance quickly. He moved up the center aisle of the train, moving with ease between the rows of seats.

He was dressed all in black, with sharply creased black

trousers, a black shirt and a black leather vest, unbuttoned except for the last button before his waist. On his head was a black hat with a wide brim, which he pulled down close to his ears, but even in the dim early morning light of the train, you could still make out some of his facial features. The young man sitting next to her also looked up and glanced at the man dressed in black, who was approaching them through the center aisle of the train.

Even though the train rolled and rocked as it moved along the tracks, he did not reach up for any handholds or assistance. His strides remained long and steady and he did not waver or even miss a step with his gait. The rocking of the train and the sway and roll of the cars caused him no loss of balance or even the slightest break in his giant strides.

The young woman studied the man in black as he strode along, and she could not help but think that although his clothes seemed so expensive and brand new, he appeared as if he was from the past, or from some bygone era in time.

Regardless, he was indeed striking in his demeanor and appearance. Even though she was a young gal, and this man seemed as if he was around her own father's age, she had no qualms about thinking how extraordinarily handsome he was. His appearance, clothes, and demeanor . . . just the way he moved captivated her.

The man had a thin, closely trimmed beard that neatly framed his face. The young woman identified the noise that alerted her to his presence because on his feet were black, sharp-tipped boots, with a metal clip on the edge that made a distinct clicking noise as he walked along the floor of the train. He walked with an air of confidence as he strode along.

You could tell that this was a gentleman that was used to traveling around, and you could easily see that he was comfortable in many different surroundings.

She continued to watch him, as did the young man next to her and she took a bit of a deep breath. When he stopped in the center aisle between the two riders' rows, he adjusted his hat and looked around. It seemed as if his mind was calculating, or if he was searching for a specific location. She watched his dark eyes and when he suddenly turned into her row; she sat back in her seat, somewhat surprised at his sudden seat selection. Even though there were many empty seats on the train this particular morning, she watched while the dark stranger selected and settled in the seat directly opposite her!

He said not a single word; he simply adjusted his hat and then stared out the window for a moment or two.

The young woman tried to force herself not to stare at the stranger in the black hat, but she found it hard not to study the man out of the corner of her eyes. He was indeed different and captivating, and suddenly, she could no longer resist glancing his way, as she caught his glance for just a fleeting moment. His deep black eyes pierced the early morning light, and when their eyes met for just a moment, she felt a slight shudder go down her spine at his rather ominous appearance.

To her astonishment, as well as the young man sitting next to her, the normally aloof, young woman, felt the sudden need to speak to the dark, quiet stranger. She normally would not say much more than a greeting, or a nod of her head, but now she suddenly and mysteriously made small talk.

She spoke rather softly, carefully watching him to gauge a reaction, "Hello, and good morning. I have grown so weary of the snowy landscapes. I long for the day when the grass will show out the window again. . .."

She forced an uneasy laugh. The ever-confident young woman found herself fascinated by the stranger in the black hat, but at the same token, aghast at her speaking to this dark and foreboding, yet handsome man.

He did not say a word, but turned his head to the side and once again stared out the window.

Now, the young woman was very uncomfortable and for just a moment, she considered packing her belongings up, grabbing her winter coat, and moving to another seat. Something unexplained kept her from doing so; it was not a specific feeling that she could pinpoint, but something inside of her compelled her to stay there and she settled back into the seat.

Once more, to her amazement, she asked the quiet stranger in the black hat, "I have not seen you riding the train before. Are you new on the commute into the city? Did you recently move to New Jersey?"

He had no reaction to her questions. He still said not a single word, but continued to stare out the window.

Not a single movement or motion.

He was the quiet stranger in the black hat.

The young woman realized the futility of any further questions, so she reached back down into her bag in order to begin to give the paperback another try. After many minutes of silence, flipping through a few pages and reading, but not paying any attention or comprehending what the words meant or conveyed, she closed the book once again in frustration.

She leaned over to place the book back in her bag when, to her amazement; the quiet stranger in the black hat suddenly spoke up and said, "The book has no appeal, eh? Perhaps the joy you seek and what is missing in your life, is contained within the pages of another book. Sometimes, we just have to have the courage to blow the dust off our mind and souls, as well as the covers of the books of our lives, then take the time to read and turn a page or two, eh?"

His words ran a cold shiver up and down her spine. She studied his face, and she thought, "Just who the hell is this guy? How did those words he just spoke, just send a ripple up and down my entire body and a whirlwind of memories in my mind?"

The way that the quiet stranger in the black hat ended his sentences with a distinct, "Eh," was a reminder to her of her father and his rather distinctive manner of speaking.

She dropped the book in the bag and looked at the quiet stranger in the black hat. But right for now, she had no words to say. Her mind was now a bit too scrambled, too scattered. She could not focus or find any words for a reply. It was rather uncomfortable for her; she was always in control, especially when it came to handsome men. The young woman, who always had it together, had been disrupted by a few sentences, spoken by a stranger sitting opposite her on a train.

She shook it off and covered up her loss of control and composure. Regaining her confidence and her New Jersey swagger, she sat back, flipped her hair, turned on the feminine charm, and said, "Well, that particular book is not exactly my style. I cannot seem to get into it, despite my best efforts. Have you read it?"

The quiet stranger in the black hat simply stared at her with those piercing black eyes; he did not answer her or say a word. He was studying her intensely, as if he was interpreting her thoughts or reading her mind. This entire episode was uncanny, but the young woman could not look away. She was not sure why.

She watched, as from underneath the wide brim of his hat, his face broke into a gentle smile.

He spoke once more, in a low, melodious voice, a voice that now contained a gentle tone, a quiet resonance to it, "No, it is not my style either. I do not read much, but when I do, I usually read boring, humorous fiction. No zombies, no violence, no murders, or end of the world. Pure Americana, with a New Jersey twist is actually my preference. It is amazing, how the words of a good book can reveal so much emotion and help you to overcome your past pain. I highly recommend you read some of the same."

Her body trembled at the words; her own thoughts conveyed to her! This must be a wild daydream! This stranger and this entire situation cannot be real.

He smiled once again, then suddenly stood up, tipped his hat to the young woman and walked briskly up the center aisle towards the front of the train. She could hear the distinct click of the metal clips on his boots as he walked farther away until he faded from her view and she heard them no longer.

The young woman bent over, held her head in her hands for a moment and she held tightly onto the edges of the seat. She could feel the young man across the aisle studying her. She steadfastly refused to show him, or anyone, any more weakness, or project any implication that the words of the quiet stranger affected her in any manner.

What, or who, was the quiet stranger in the black hat? How did he reveal to her the actual thoughts that she hid in her own heart? She recovered, and now she was a bit puzzled as to where the stranger was going, or why he suddenly left, because a glance at her watch told her that they were still about ten minutes out from any scheduled train stop.

The young man next to her glanced over, smiled and shrugged his shoulders; as if to indicate that he too was not sure where the man was going, because it was not as if he could get off the moving train.

In fact, she was not sure how he actually got on the train in the first place.

The young woman leaned back. Now she was determined to remove these strange experiences and nagging thoughts from out of her mind. She needed to concentrate on her upcoming workday. She had important meetings this morning and it was time to lose the pain of the past and think about the day ahead. This was all so strange . . . these embers of the flames of the past, flickering in front of her, warming her soul in a very strange manner.

It might have been her imagination, but it seemed as if for a few seconds, the train slowed on a long curve. It slowed to a point where it was very noticeable. She made a note of that and vowed to check on another ride, if the train normally slowed in that location, or if she just never noticed it before.

It was another successful workday for the young woman. The meetings went well, her management was well pleased with her performance and she continued to make points to climb the company ladder. After the meeting, she played all the managers and some clients, like fine violins over a business lunch, smiling and captivating them all with her intelligence, her beauty and her business sense.

She knew that she was now well on her way, an executive on the road to success!

Yet, those empty feelings always returned. Money, smiles, fine clothes, top-shelf cocktails at lunch and drooling men did not remove the emptiness from her life or from her mind.

The hustle and bustle and excitement of the workday was lost on the dull ride back home, out of the city, back to New Jersey.

Off she went, in the opposite way of the ride in . . . over and over, day after day, the same routine. She sat reflectively on the ride home and wondered where it all was taking her.

Yet this ride back home was different. She still could not forget the bizarre encounter and nagging thought of the words of the quiet stranger in the black hat. She wondered if he would show up on the return ride into Jersey. He did not.

At her apartment that night, she prepared some dinner, watched some television and listened to some music. She kept the music softly playing in the background; it was a way to interrupt the silence.

She needed to retire early. The train pulled into the station at the first light of dawn and sleeping for weary New Jersey commuters occurred on the train or on the weekends.

It was a tedious life.

She climbed in bed, set the alarm, and rolled over.

She tossed, turned, and rolled back and forth, pulling the covers over her, twisting and turning. The look on the face of the quiet stranger in the black hat repeated over and over in her mind. Despite the long day that she had experienced, sleep would not come easily, or in fact, at all.

His words would not stop speaking to her in her mind.

"The book has no appeal, eh? Perhaps the joy you seek and what is missing in your life, is contained within the pages of another book. Sometimes, we just have to have the courage to blow the dust off our mind and souls, as well as the covers of the books of our lives, and then take the time to read and turn a page or two, eh?"

A thousand dreams of her father and her childhood floated everywhere, and they chased her into every corner of her room, flashing in her mind, as if they were a beacon of joy, hope, dreams and love.

It was more than she could stand; she finally tore the covers off and apprehensively walked into her spare bedroom. Suddenly, she no longer had the emotional power to withstand it; she flipped the overhead light on and tore open the door to a spare closet. She violently moved box after box out of the way until she found the one in which she sought. She pulled and tugged the box free and moved it to the center of the room.

She opened the top and stared inside.

Picking up the first book, she blew the dust off the cover and watched it scatter in the dim light of the bedroom.

Dust of the ages now scattered to memories.

She sat cross-legged on the floor of the bedroom and

opened the first book that she grabbed out of the box, which was a Christmas book. She ran her fingers over the name of the author on the cover page.

Her father's name.

She read the foreword aloud to no one and after doing so; it was then that she realized. Contained here were the answers that she had been seeking. They were a secret view at her father's soul. The pages held all of it tightly within their grasp. His writing captivated her. She could hear her father's voice and soul speaking to her from the words on the pages. His hopes, his dreams, his life, his love, his insight.

She was a part of this too; she thumbed through each page; she read on and on for hours upon hours. She read of his adventures, his victories, and of his defeats. She read of his courage, his fears, of the energy of his invulnerability and, on the opposite side, the total exposure of his innocence.

Everything hidden carefully within the seemingly endless pages of fictional humor, wild characters, and deception was a quiet facade of someone that she loved so deeply that she could not even measure it.

A man who hid his true feelings under that same facade.

He created characters that he hid behind, characters to shield his own emotions, his own pain, his joy and, at times, his deep despair. Characters, which helped to show how much he loved his life, family, his religion and God, and his relatives, and friends. His words reflected how strongly spiritual he actually was, how he firmly believed that everything had a purpose and was under God's control. He could not say all of this with his spoken words; however, on the printed page, it all became clear.

Her father grew up lean and mean, in a tough, urban New Jersey neighborhood. He never forgot how special that old neighborhood really turned out to be. No matter what his upbringing was, he grew to achieve more success than she had ever realized.

Success, in more ways than was readily apparent with dollar signs.

Her father lived an extraordinary life, had special friends whom he loved deeply, he mixed with his daily life, some very special people and he had the insight to detail it, in a very special way.

She laughed until her belly hurt, at his wild humor and hilarious adventures, she cried at the tenderness of his words and she rode the waves of endless memories and emotions. Then she shared within his words the quiet times of his loneliness and his despair. She recognized some tales from stories that he had told her and her brother when they were children. She knew her own relatives, who he brought back to life on these pages, and she felt the special and unique companionship of his lifelong friends that he mentioned.

She cried at the incredible love which he had for her dear mother, for her, and for her brother.

It was as if she had entered a special back door of his mind. It was all a magnificent outpouring of a chronicle of her father's life.

She glanced at one of the dedications of the Christmas compilation and she read it aloud, "To—to—to. . .." Her voice trailed off. She could not even speak her own name, but she replaced it with, "Me." Amongst a rain of tears, she continued, "Because you always wanted to read my serious side."

She closed the book and smiled.

There were no zombies, there was no violence, or end of the world. There was something quite different within the pages she had read. It was a simple journey into the past, into her own father's life and into what was a part of her life, too. There was something inside those pages in which she knew she had missed more than she ever knew or realized.

There, within, she found her father once more.

Maybe he had made some mistakes. Maybe she had made some too. He had tried and failed at certain things, but she knew one thing, he loved her and she loved him too. All it took was the courage to turn the right pages, just as the quiet stranger in the black hat had told her, for her, and maybe, for all of them to realize it.

She put the Christmas book down and picked up another one.

A novel, a long, long novel.

She took it proudly in her hands, went downstairs to her favorite chair in the living room, turned on a reading lamp, and settled in.

She already knew she would be calling in sick to work tomorrow.

She read for hours upon hours, and she could not put the book down. She never realized the depth of his talent to tell a story, and his book stole her heart and filled her with joy. When the dawn was breaking and the early morning sunlight peeked over the shades of her apartment, she finally reached the end and read aloud to the early morning streams of light, the closing words of the book.

"I thought to myself, how I just may embrace the modern age, but I will never forget the memories of the old times. . .. Indeed not, my dear reader. I can assure you that I will never, ever, forget."

She closed the book with tears rolling down her cheeks and she said, "And neither will your daughter, my dear Father, neither will, I."

She jumped out of her chair, ran to the telephone, looked up a number on a pad, and dialed the telephone.

It was early, but she knew he would answer.

He always does.

A few weeks later, the young woman stood on a platform waiting for that same train.

This time, it was very different.

There was delight in her heart. It was time for her to go home.

Spring now grew closer and the cold wait for the train to arrive next to the platform was becoming less numbing. This was the last day she was going to do this; she had given her employer a notice of resignation a few weeks earlier, and as a result, she now suffered through endless meetings with her management, who continually attempted to talk her out of resigning her position.

"You are a rising star here! Are you crazy to leave this once in a lifetime, fantastic opportunity behind you? You will be earning a fortune in another year or so!"

It was a common cry that meant nothing to her anymore.

She had another dream in mind.

She was going to become a writer.

It was time to follow her heart and to be happy.

"When life boils down to the final moments, if you can look back and say that you were happy, then you will never have any regrets. The only person that truly knows that you are happy is the person whom you see in the mirror every, single day. That person is the one person, who is impossible to fool."

My goodness, her father could write such powerful words. Yes, she had made her mind up; she was going to become a writer. There, she would write of her loves, her hopes, her dreams and her desires. She would write of her adventures. She would write of her father and of her mother. In her mind, she had already formulated stories to include the wonderful people she encountered and would continue to encounter along the way, story lines of her failures and of her successes.

Sorry, there will be no zombies, no blood or gore, no violence, no end of the world, or sappy, romantic novels filled with meaningless, sexual interludes. She had vowed to write only simple stories. Stories laced with humor and emotion in all the right spots, boring, humorous fiction, with a New Jersey twist. True Americana! She will also add a touch of sentiment and tenderness, which will tell of ordinary people who live ordinary lives.

Well, sort of ordinary lives and sort of ordinary people.

She felt that she had a superb role model to follow. She might starve, but she knew whom she could call for advice at any time of the day or night.

He would always answer. He always does.

While she stood there smiling at the thought of her plans, she was surprised to feel a gentle touch upon her shoulder.

She turned around to stare directly into the eyes of the quiet stranger in the black hat.

She did not know why or how, but she always knew that someday he would appear once again in her life. She knew that he always does.

This time, he looked a little different. Studying him closely in the light, she could not help but think that his resemblance to her father was uncanny. He smiled at her, and she smiled back.

Under the wide rim of the black hat, she saw his eyes light up, and he spoke, "I see that you found the correct pages to turn, eh? As your father would write, there is nothing but blue skies ahead of you now."

The young woman laughed and said, "I do not know who you are, and perhaps, I am better off not knowing, but thank you for your advice. He also wrote that the beauty you see in a sunset is really a promise of hope and joy for a new day. I love those words. Those words are my favorite words that he ever wrote. You see, a few days ago, I spoke to my father for the first time in many years. When we spoke, I told him how beautiful those words are and how special he is in my heart. I also told him that I allowed the sun to set upon an old dream, with the promise of a new one."

The young woman looked up towards the sky and then

back into the quiet stranger's wonderful, dark eyes.

She told him, "It seems as if, somehow, somewhere, either in the past or right now, that we made a contract together. Thank you for caring and fulfilling your end of the agreement. I promise that I will fulfill mine too."

He only nodded. She took that to be his reply.

She smiled and asked, "I guess that you deal in healing broken hearts?"

The quiet stranger in the black hat stood up taller. She realized that he was a very large man! He was as tall as her father was.

He gently shook his head as he softly said, "No, I alone, cannot heal broken hearts. I can only remind people of what they already know in their hearts, in their souls, and in their minds. Think of me as some old photographs and memories kept in a box, or a stack of passionate love letters tied up with strings, and carefully hidden away by lovers in dusty drawers . . . forgotten reminders of the past that are suddenly rediscovered. I represent the truth that for whatever reason, we sometimes choose to forget, or are too afraid to admit."

The quiet stranger in the black hat stepped backwards a step or two. He tilted his head, and under the brim of his hat, she could still see his dark eyes piercing the early morning light. He grew intense, and it seemed as if he was searching for special words, or he was searching her mind.

The words finally arrived, along with just a gentle glint in his dark eyes. "Above all, I deal in love, joy, hope, and memories, as well as blowing off the dust of the ages."

He tipped his hat, smiled, turned and walked briskly away. The young woman smiled and watched until he left her view, and she could no longer hear the click of the metal tips of his boots on the walkway.

THE END

Epilogue

Life goes drifting on by, and while we run along with it, often, life captures us in its fierce currents of change and in the undertow of turmoil. Sometimes, we feel lost in the vicious sea of life, drowning hopelessly, no one to save us, no one to care, no hope on the horizon. Everything is lost, until a calm wave arrives; a wave, which picks us up out of the violence, out of the turbulence and carries us safely back to shore.

Those waves, which come along, are the ones we all look for during the many desperate times in our lives. The ones that save us, or show us the truth that we do not have the courage to confront, or are too afraid of admitting, the ones that restore us and keep us all going.

Those waves come in many shapes and forms. Often, they are words, or they are religion or hope. Sometimes, they are special people, or emotions, or just pure love.

We can only hope someday to understand it all. Why they arrive, who they are or who actually sends them.

Until then, we all stand together, while watching and waiting, somewhere, at the heart of the sunrise of a new day.

We all watch and we wait for the day, when either collectively or individually, we all will have the chance to see him tip his hat, smile, turn, and walk briskly away.

Together, we will all smile too and we will watch.

We all watch until he leaves our view and we can no longer hear the click of the metal tips of his boots on the walkway.

ABOUT THE AUTHOR

If you ask Paul John Hausleben, he will tell you that he is not an author, he is just a storyteller. His mission is to continue to write and tell stories to warm your heart, make you laugh, and sometimes make you cry, just a little. Most of all, he deals in memories, and helps you to remember the good times of your own life, and the special people who touched you along the way. Paul was born and raised in Paterson, and then nearby Haledon, New Jersey, and began writing at an early age. He revisited a writing career later in his life, and he now is the author of a number of novels, compilations, short stories and audio and video works. Most of his work touches upon nostalgic remembrances of simpler times, and tells the stories of heartfelt, humorous, and special human relationships. Other than writing, among many careers both paid and unpaid, he is a former semi-professional hockey goaltender, a music fan and music reviewer, an avid sports fan, photographer and amateur radio operator. He now resides in Somewhere, U.S.A., but his heart always remains along Belmont Avenue in good old Paterson, and Haledon, New Jersey.

Titles by the same author that you also may enjoy:

The Time Bomb in The Cupboard and Other Adventures of Harry and Paul.

The Night Always Comes, Another story from the Adventures of Harry and Paul.

Reunion, A sequel to the Night Always Comes and Another story from the Adventures of Harry and Paul

The Autumn Collection

The Christmas Tree and Other Christmas Stories. Tales for a Christmas Evening

Crows on a High Wire

The Miracle Tree, Another story from the Adventures of Harry and Paul

The Summer Collection

The Time Bomb in The Cupboard and Other Adventures of Harry and Paul.
Special Edition

The Return of the Quiet Stranger in the Black Hat

You may write to the author at ctte27@gmail.com

Published by God Bless the Keg Publishing
Somewhere, U.S.A.

You may write to the publisher at
Godblessthekegpublishing@gmail.com

"Life's simple pleasures are so often the best ones!"

www.ingramcontent.com/pod-product-compliance
Lightning Source LLC
LaVergne TN
LVHW051000080826
845145LV00009B/2375

* 9 7 8 0 9 9 0 6 9 7 9 0 9 *